PARDNERS OF THE BADLANDS

PARDNERS OF THE BADLANDS

Bliss Lomax

GUNSMOKE

First published in the UK by Muller

This hardback edition 2010
by BBC Audiobooks Ltd
by arrangement with
Golden West Literary Agency

ISBN 978 1 408 46248 5

British Library Cataloguing in Publication Data available.

Printed and bound in Great Britain by
CPI Antony Rowe, Chippenham and Eastbourne

PARDNERS OF THE BADLANDS

Chapter One

"WAAL, TIE me down if that ain't somethin'!"
Grumpy Gibbs declared with a loud snort of disgust as he
viewed the preparations going forward here on the bank of
the Green River. Half a mile below the little Wyoming town
of Black Forks, the Thaddeus Hammersley Expedition was
outfitting for its well-publicized attempt to run the canyons
of the Green and the Colorado. The little man's tone had
never been crustier. "I've chased outlaws and rustlers and
slapped down the ears of more'n one killer in my time, but
I'll be hornswoggled if I'm fool enough to want any of this
dish! Look at them boats! Flat as pumpkin seeds! They're too
big and too wide to git through rapids like they'll find down
in the Canyon of Lodore or Desolation. Why, Rainbow, they
won't be fit for kindlin' wood by the time they hit the Gun-
nison Valley!"

A smile touched Rainbow Ripley's lean, bronzed face. Dif-
ferences of opinion between his partner and himself were too
common to cause him any concern. They had traveled too far
and been through too much gun smoke together for that. In
the present instance, Rainbow knew that the little man was
only blowing off steam that he had been storing up for several weeks.

Rainbow had received a letter from Professor Thaddeus
Hammersley, in New York City, seeking to engage their
services for the long and hazardous voyage down the mighty
Colorado. The idea had appealed to Ripley, but Grumpy had
raised a score of objections.

"Don't agitate yourself; we're just looking," Rainbow told
his partner. They had ridden down from Judge Carver's
ranch where they had been taking things easy for a month.

3

"You can see that Hammersley isn't going about this in any two-by-four way. He's got a dozen men here already, and the party from New York, the scientists and photographers, won't be showing up for another week."

"Yeah," Grumpy grumbled. "He's got enough stuff here to outfit an army. D'yuh mean to tell me he's goin' to cart all them boxes and bales of grub and instruments through stretches of bad water like Hell's Half Mile? An' what's he need 'em for?"

"He expects to lose some boats, I suppose. That's been the story with every party that has tried to run the canyons. You know how it was with the Bancroft Expedition. They had all their grub in one boat. It was smashed up in Disaster Falls. They starved to death—all but one who crawled out to the old Uinta Agency."

"And you still want a helpin' of this dish?" Grumpy growled. He shook his head violently. "Not for me! Ain't nuthin' for this Hammersley to discover. Major Powell did that thirty years ago. Took all the pitchers and learned all there is to know. There ain't no sense in doin' it all over again jest to be able to brag that you did it. An' takin' wimmen along! Two of 'em, you say?"

"Yeah. Miss Thane, Hammersley's ward, and a Miss Wattress, the painter. You read the letter."

"The man's mad!" Grumpy insisted stubbornly. "I don't claim to know these rivers, but I've seen 'em from the cliffs and I know what they can do to you. When this bunch gits through the Flamin' Gorge, there won't be no turnin' back. They'll have to go on, then, whether they like it or not. But that don't mean we got to invite ourselves along. We'd have one foot in the grave and the other on a banana peel before we'd gone ten miles!"

Grumpy's vehemence sounded familiar enough, but Rainbow caught an undercurrent that swung him around in his saddle. Though he was the younger of the two by ten years, he never failed to remind himself that a great measure of the success they had enjoyed as stock and range detectives was

4

due to the doughty little man's loyalty, courage, and stubborn, unbending will. After a long glance at that grizzled, hard-bitten face he said: "I thought you were just blowing off, but you mean this, don't you?"

"I shore do!" was the flinty answer. "I read about Hammersley goin' to look for mineral deposits and that daughter of his, or whatever she is, takin' pitchers in natural colors, but it don't mean nuthin' to me. We're range detectives, not a couple of water rats. I tell you, I've seen these canyons all the way from the Flamin' Gorge down to Robbers' Roost, an' I ain't got no hankerin' to see any more of 'em. Git into trouble and there ain't no one to help you—not even Injuns. You're cut off from everythin'. There ain't more'n four or five places between here and Lee's Ferry where you kin crawl out, and you ain't got no place when you do."

Fifty yards downstream two of the men ran one of the shallow, wide-beamed boats into the river and deliberately upset it. The strange-looking craft bobbed to the surface immediately and, when it was easily righted, appeared as buoyant as ever. The men then tried to sink the boat, but it refused to stay down.

"Waal, that's shore purty good," Grumpy acknowledged grudgingly. "Those boats will pack a load."

"Airtight compartments," Rainbow told him. "These men Hammersley's got to handle them seem to know their business. The judge told me he'd heard some of them were from Alaska."

"They're a tough-looking bunch, if you ask me," growled the little man. "If any of 'em are from Alaska, I bet they left in a hurry, for one reason or another."

Rainbow laughed. "Suppose we talk to 'em."

Without waiting for Grumpy's answer he kneed his horse and moved down the bank toward the tents. The little man followed, growling to himself. When they were within a few feet of the piles of boxes and crates, an armed man suddenly stepped out and ordered them to turn back.

"We ain't askin' for visitors," he said gruffly, "and I ain't tellin' yuh twicet." He tapped the rifle he carried over his arm significantly.

Rainbow's lips tightened at this unwarranted hospitality. "That's putting it up to us a little rough, ain't it?" he queried, searching the face before him. It seemed to be all slitted eyes and chin. "Have you got something here to hide?"

"Naw, we ain't got nuthin' to hide," was the surly answer, "but we gotta lot of equipment spready around here and we ain't takin' no chance of it turnin' up missin'."

Several of the other men ran up, their attitude equally threatening. Rainbow had to agree with Grumpy that they were a tough-looking bunch.

"What's the matter, Ginger?" one growled. "Are these gents givin' you an argyment?"

"I'm wonderin' about that," the man with the long chin sneered, balancing his rifle lightly in the crook of his arm.

"If it's an argyment yo're lookin' for it's right under yore nose, mister!" Grumpy burst out. This business had got under his skin, and he pushed forward, mad as a hornet. "We ain't got no fault to find with bein' told to turn back and keep out, but I'm danged if we're goin' to be treated like a couple of hoss thieves. I'll have you know there's a chance we may be goin' down the canyons with this party. I'm Gibbs, and this is my pardner, Rainbow Ripley."

The men exchanged a quick glance, but Grumpy's attention remained fixed on Ginger. Something in the depths of the latter's narrowed eyes told him the names were not unknown to the man.

"You may be all right, but I don't know you from Adam," Ginger said flatly. "An' I ain't had no instructions to be on the lookout for you. If yo're friends of the perfessor's you'll have to show me some papers."

"Let him take a look at them letters from Hammersley," Grumpy told his companion.

"No, we won't bother with that," said Rainbow. "We'll wait until Hammersley shows up. We'll be at the hotel in Black Forks if anyone wants to find us."

Swinging his horse around, he started for town. Grumpy let fly a last retort and then took after Rainbow, wondering if a slug in the back might not stop the two of them before they got very far.

"Say, what was the idee lettin' me down thataway?" he demanded fiercely when he came abreast of Rainbow. "We could've made that gent eat his flip talk!"

Ripley shook his head. "I'm afraid not. We didn't have anything for him to chew on. Those letters are in my room, up at the ranch. But speaking of ideas, what was that crack you made about there being a chance of our going along with that outfit?"

"Talk! Jest talk!" Grumpy snorted. "You know dang well I was only tryin' to make that gent hunt his hole! Laugh if you want to! I may give you one that'll split yore sides when we hit town."

They were in Black Forks a few minutes later.

"Hold on!" the little man exclaimed as Rainbow headed for the hotel. "I wanta drop into the sheriff's office for a minute. You come along."

They found Sheriff Rod Effingham preparing to go home for supper when they walked in.

"Heard you was in town," the lawman greeted them. "Somethin' on your minds?"

"Rod, do you keep yore old Wanted Men notices?" Grumpy asked.

"Shore! Got a stack of 'em filed away. You want to run through 'em?"

"If you don't mind. Git 'em out and then run along. We'll jest sit here a few minutes, if it's all right with you."

For a quarter of an hour Grumpy ran over the old handbills before a sharp grunt of satisfaction escaped him. "Jest as I thought!" he exclaimed. "Lissen to this: 'William—alias Ginger—Revell. Wanted in connection with robbery of Great Northern train at Scott's Station, Montana. Now take a look at that face! There's our friend with the big chin!"

Across the bottom of the notice Rod had penciled: "Two years Montana pen."

"He ain't been out long," Rainbow observed soberly. "I wondered if you recognized him."

"Huh?" Grumpy demanded with a crestfallen air. "You mean to say you knew?"

"It's pretty hard to forget a face like that. Wasn't it your idea that Revell could have told us something about that case we were on up in the Judith Basin, four years ago, if we could have caught up with him?"

Grumpy could only shake his puzzled head. "Rainbow, why would a crook like Ginger Revell git himself mixed up with this Hammersley Expedition? What does it mean?"

"I don't know, but if the good doctor has any more like Revell in that bunch he better have someone along to look out for him."

"Mebbe he had," growled Grumpy, "but that don't mean it's got to be us!"

"No," Rainbow admitted, leading the way across the street to the hotel.

He found a telegram there for him.

"Waal?" the little man demanded uneasily as Ripley read the message. "Who's it from? Hammersley?"

"It's from Tom Moran, the general manager of the Rocky Mountain Shortline. He wants us to meet him at the railroad offices in Platte City, Colorado, on Wednesday. Important, he says."

A wide grin spread over Grumpy's weather-beaten face. "Waal!" he declared with relief. "That sounds like a job! Our kind of a job! You'll go, of course?"

"I'll have to go." Rainbow could not hold back a grin as he saw Grumpy perk up. "Tom Moran has come through for us too many times to let him down. I don't know what he wants, but it won't do any harm to hear what he's got to say."

"Now yo're talkin', by gravy! If we're goin' to be in Platte City on Wednesday, Rainbow, we gotta grab the train east in

Green River tonight. That'll jest give us time to git supper here and make tracks."

'The little man was actually garrulous as they ate. That was usually the case when his spirits were riding high. On the way north to Green River, however, he fell silent and had nothing to say for miles.

"What's the matter with you?" Rainbow demanded finally. "You've closed up like a clam."

"Rainbow, I bin thinkin'. Hammersley don't know he's got a crook like Revell, an' mebbe others, workin' for him, does he?"

"Well, hardly——"

"Then why has he bin offerin' us a job? What's he want us for? If it ain't pertection he's thinkin' of, then what is it? Jest how was we to be of any use to him?"

Rainbow slowed his horse to a walk and stared at the little man without knowing how to answer. "I don't know," he admitted frankly. "I never thought of it that way. Hammersley is a rich man. I don't suppose the money he'd be paying us would mean anything to him, but I can't tell you why he wants us."

Grumpy nodded to himself grimly. "It might not be a bad idea to find out," he muttered. "This thing don't smell right to me!"

Chapter Two

ACROSS the continent in New York City a conference was taking place that pleasant April evening in the home of Professor Thaddeus Hammersley, in Gramercy Park South. The conversation would have thoroughly enlightened Grumpy Gibbs had he been able to put an ear to it.

Though the residents of that quiet and delightful section

9

of the great city had no closer acquaintance with Thaddeus Hammersley than they were able to gain from reading from time to time of his explorations and adventures in various parts of the world, they accepted him as an illustrious neighbor and had long since ceased to remark on his unexpected comings and goings, always in the close company of a stocky, unsmiling Japanese who was reported to be his secretary and assistant.

When Professor Hammersley was in residence, his visitors were not infrequent, and as might have been expected, they were often of a type to quicken and excite the imagination. The rocky-faced, hard-jawed man with whom Hammersley was seated in his study this evening was no exception. By the cut of his clothes he was a Westerner and, judging from the air of authority he gave himself, a person of some consequence, in his own mind at least. Across his heavily carved desk Hammersley regarded him approvingly.

"You have carried out my instructions to the letter," he said. "I knew I had not made any mistake in selecting you for this . . . er . . . shall we say . . . enterprise?"

"I've gathered a bunch of men out there who know their way around," the other replied. "Boat or saddle is all the same to them. You'll find them handy enough with their guns and fists. The law's had grudges against most of them, but you said that didn't matter——"

"Not at all, Brant!" Hammersley assured him. "I need desperate men who'll see this through no matter what it costs. This will not be the first time I've done what others said was impossible. As I told you when I last saw you in Cheyenne, I've worked out every detail of this undertaking as carefully as though it were a scientific problem." He smiled. "I don't mind telling you I have found it far more interesting than such dry stuff as that. With the proper assistance from you, I can't fail!"

His piercing black eyes had begun to burn so brightly that the rest of his face seemed to be only a dead mask. It was a peculiarity that Samson Brant had noticed before, and he caught himself wondering if Hammersley were really sane. His glance ran over this magnificently appointed room, with its case on case of rare specimens and beautifully carved jade and ivory, souvenirs from the four corners of the earth. To Brant it seemed a strange setting in which to be discussing a crime of such magnitude and daring that his own past criminal activities faded into insignificance, but it was at once a hundredfold more incredible and fantastic to realize that Thaddeus Hammersley, the rich, world-famous scientist of sterling reputation, was the mastermind of the scheme; that for months he had devoted himself to its accomplishment with an open purse and all the vigor and Machiavellian shrewdness of his fifty-odd years.

"It is a very interesting room," Hammersley broke in on Brant's musing with a thin edge of sarcasm. "I should be delighted to show it to you sometime. But we were speaking of the co-operation I am to expect from you, Brant——"

"You had your answer to that some months back," his visitor said sullenly. "You left me no choice."

"Exactly," the professor declared without raising his voice. "I'm glad you understood me. I don't expect any loyalty from you beyond what I can purchase, and I mean purchase with money and threat of exposure. But you are no fool, Brant; it will pay you well to carry out my orders without question. Your fake irrigation schemes and mining ventures haven't netted you anything. Principally because you are inclined to be too greedy. In the four months I was in Montana last fall I saw enough of you and your scheming to understand your limitations. The only reason you escaped going to prison for that last fiasco was my deciding not to testify against you——"

"Do we have to go into that again?" Brant demanded with a show of anger. "I haven't gone this far with you to back out now. I'll stick till this job is done, but you might as well understand right now that I'm not going all the way down the river with you. This man Utah Jim McBride, who I've hired to guide us, claims he's been down the Green and

Colorado as far as the Granite Gorge. It's his opinion that we'll be mighty lucky to get the boats, with all that beam, through Lodore. I know why the boats had to be wide, but I'm not going to risk my neck in them for nothing. McBride says if we try Marble Canyon or Granite Gorge we'll never come out alive."

"He's right," Hammersley said without hesitation. He got up and walked to a window overlooking the park. He was an immensely tall man. With his bushy gray hair and hawk-like nose he was an arresting figure. He turned to Brant suddenly. "I think I can safely predict that the Hammersley Expedition will be a complete fiasco as far as reaching the Colorado is concerned. Our work will have been accomplished long before then. The rest will be just a matter of continuing until no suspicion can attach to us. I predict a series of minor misfortunes that will end in abandonment of the undertaking."

"That means throwing away between eight to ten thousand dollars in wages and equipment." Brant could only shake his head admiringly at the cold-blooded audacity of the man. "There must be a better way."

"There *is* no other way!" Professor Hammersley said with flat finality. "A million dollars' worth of raw silk rolling across this country on an average of once a month, and it's never been molested. And only because until now no one has been able to conceive of any way of making off with even part of it!" His eyes were burning again and unconsciously he raised his voice. "Raw silk, hard to identify! As salable as government bonds! We're playing for a big stake, Mr. Brant! My investment is nothing!"

The door opened quietly and Saburo Itchi, the Japanese, stepped into the room. Brant gave a warning cough.

"We have no secrets from Itchi," Hammersley told him. "As we go along you will discover that the success of our plans will depend in no little degree on his contribution. Nevertheless you will address him as just my secretary. Itchi, this is Samson Brant. You will remember him from Montana."

"Yes, I identified him by the smell of his cigar." The

Japanese turned a pair of blank, inscrutable eyes that never gave any hint of what he was thinking to Brant. "I have been going over your expense account, Mr. Brant. There is an item that puzzles me: One hundred dollars for 'sugar.'"

"I got a man I wanted out of the jug. Gass Labelle, if you want his name. We can use him." Brant's mouth took on a harder angle. "Why?" he whipped out. "Is there any question about it?"

Little Saburo Itchi met the query with an expressionless yellow face. "No," he murmured. "If he is a good man I would say you got a bargain. You will excuse me, please."

Bowing to Professor Hammersley, Itchi crossed the study to his office. Through the open door he could follow the conversation in the next room. This role of secretary and humble assistant which he was satisfied to play, though his achievements in science rated him as the equal of men whose names were famous, was not the usual case of Japanese duplicity biding its time. In the nine years since Itchi had accompanied Thaddeus Hammersley into the deserts of Outer Mongolia he had learned how to give himself such perfect expression through the mind of the other that he had fallen a victim to his own experiment and come completely under the older man's spell.

"What about these other people you're taking along?" Brant was asking. "What are we to do with them?"

In his office Itchi shook his head. "Such an irrelevant question. He has the mind of a child," he said softly to himself.

"I shall find a way to separate the sheep from the goats," Professor Hammersley answered with a mirthless laugh. "The mouth of the Yampa River might be an excellent place. We'll be camped there overnight."

"But this ward of yours—Miss Thane?" persisted Brant.

The professor had come back to his desk. He leaned back in his chair and gave the man a long, cold glance. "Miss Thane is a very courageous young woman," he said softly. "Suppose you leave her to me. I don't believe in becoming emotional about these things."

"I see you don't!" Brant whipped out. "There's something about you that's beginning to give me the creeps. You can't murder half a dozen people in those canyons or anywhere else and get away with it."

"We will have trouble with that man before we are through," the listening Itchi told himself. "We shall very likely have to dispose of him also—quietly."

"Murder is a very unpleasant-sounding word, Brant," the professor remarked. "I wasn't considering anything so crude and unnecessary. But accidents are not uncommon on such a trip. I think you understand me."

"Yeah!" Brant dropped his waterlogged cigar into an ash tray and sat there meeting Hammersley's piercing regard without flinching. "That's a game two can play at, Professor. Don't let your accidents include me. I'm willing to take a little pushing around now because there's nothing I can do about it. But the minute we lay hands on that train there won't be any more of this pot-calling-the-kettle-black business. I'll have too much on you for that. I advise you and your friend Mr. Itchi to remember it."

Hammersley pretended to take it lightly. "That's a very interesting observation and true, of course." He examined his carefully tended nails for a moment. "Fortunately our need of each other will preclude any treachery. I'll make sure of that, and I know you will do the same."

"All right," Brant muttered. "Just so we understand each other. If there's nothing more to be talked over I'll go back to the hotel."

"There's the little matter of the law," said the professor. "An army of United States marshals, sheriffs, and railroad detectives will take the trail a few hours after the news breaks. I don't expect suspicion to be directed to us, but I haven't stopped there. You've heard, I daresay, of Rainbow Ripley and Gibbs, his partner."

Brant's head came up sharply. "The range detectives? What about them?"

"I've written Ripley several letters offering to meet his own terms if he and Gibbs will accompany us——"

"Are you crazy?" Samson Brant cried, leaping to his feet. "That's just the same as asking for twenty years in Leavenworth! You can't pull the wool over their eyes! That pair is too smart"

"That's precisely why I want them with us, Brant. Having them along will be killing two birds with one stone. It will not only make it impossible for the Rocky Mountain Shortline to hire them, but their very presence with us will mean a clean bill of health with the law. Depend on it that I'll arrange things so that they see and hear nothing."

"Now I know you're mad!" raged Brant. "Of all the preposterous things I ever heard of, this takes the cake!" He banged the desk with his huge fist and was catching his breath for a fresh outburst when Itchi hurried into the room.

"Gentlemen, Hendricks, the butler, is at the door," he warned. And to the professor: "I believe Miss Thane has just returned."

"All right," Hammersley murmured. "Tell Hendricks to show her in. She'll enjoy meeting our visitor. You will find my ward deeply interested in the expedition, Brant."

The rocky-faced man straightened his tie and produced a fresh cigar. He bit off the end with a savage clashing of teeth. "There's no fool like an educated one, Hammersley! You'll wish you had more horse sense and less brains if you stick to your plan of taking that pair with us!"

"I'm sure it will work out," the other said. His hearty laugh was meant for the pretty, dark-haired girl who had just stepped into the room rather than for the big man across the desk. "Here is Miss Thane now!" He got to his feet and advanced to meet her. "I was hoping you would be home early, Karen. I have a little surprise for you. This is Mr. Samson Brant, the mining expert, who has been arranging things for us in the West. Mr. Brant, this is my ward, Miss Karen Thane."

"Mr. Brant!" Karen exclaimed, her voice warm with interest. "Uncle has spoken of you so often. He tells me we are to leave a week from tomorrow."

Brant nodded. "You'll find everything ready for you when you arrive. The boats came the day before I left and I had them put into the water at once. The river is still high, but another ten days should take care of that."

"I'm so anxious to be out there," Karen told him. "I know the canyons are beautiful even in black and white. It's quite thrilling to be the first person to photograph them in color."

Karen had many questions to ask. Brant answered them as best he could, with a word now and then from the professor. By all the moral standards Samson Brant was a crook and a blackleg, but the fresh young loveliness of this girl touched some forgotten streak of decency in him and, knowing what lay ahead of her, he had to drive himself to meet her eyes. When Hammersley said, "I'm afraid we've kept Mr. Brant long enough! He was about to leave when you came in," Brant fell in with the suggestion gladly and made his escape. The professor walked to the door with him and made an appointment for the following morning.

When Hammersley returned to the study he found the Japanese awaiting him.

"The man is a fool, Doctor," said Itchi. "He will prove most difficult."

"There are no ideal accomplices, Itchi," Hammersley murmured, gathering up some papers. "Brant has a certain amount of animal courage and caution that will be useful to us. We shall permit him to have his way—or pretend to – until we have no further need of him."

"By then he will be really dangerous. It will be necessary to remove him—permanently."

"Naturally." The professor glanced at the clock. "Almost nine. We shall have to be leaving. I promised Jim Darwin I would be present to hear him read his paper on the pre-historic Mammalia of the Southwest this evening."

Itchi bowed. "We shall go at once. By the way, Doctor, you were not impressed by what Brant had to say regarding the two detectives—Rainbow Ripley and Gibbs?"

"Impressed?" Hammersley rasped. "From the first I realized how dangerous those men might be to our plans. I didn't need Brant to tell me. Because they are so dangerous is the best reason in the world why we should have them where we can watch them."

"An excellent theory," the Japanese agreed. "But some unforeseen circumstance beyond our control might arouse their suspicions———"

"We shall know how to deal with them in any case, my friend! We are not fettered by the frustrations and inhibitions of the emotion-weakened criminal mind." He quoted an ancient law of the East: " 'Your death is my life.' We shall remember it no matter who gets in our way."

Professor Hammersley was once again only giving voice to the other's unexpressed will. Itchi was not completely satisfied, however. "A trifling mistake, Doctor, would spell disaster———"

"Disaster for them!" Hammersley's tone was cold and stony. "Immediate disaster!"

"Of course," murmured Itchi, his high cheekbones casting a ghastly shadow across his yellow face as he bent down and switched off the desk lamp. "Dr. Darwin's paper should be very interesting."

Chapter Three

No. 3 WAS OVER an hour late when she rolled into Platte City on Wednesday evening. Tom Moran, the general manager of the road, hurried over to the division offices at once. He found Rainbow and Grumpy waiting for him. They had been in town since noon.

"I'm glad you stuck around," said Moran, shaking hands with them. "I expected to be here this morning, but I got held up at the last minute as I was leaving Denver. Pat Garner, our chief of detectives, came in with me. He'll be over as soon as he grabs a bite to eat. You boys had your supper?"

"Two hours ago," Rainbow told him.

"Good! We can sit here and talk then. You fixed so you can handle a job?"

"Yep," Grumpy answered at once. "Jest waitin' for somethin' to turn up."

"You're pretty quick on the trigger with that," observed Rainbow. "Suppose you let me put in a word. We've had a job offered us, Tom: this Hammersley Expedition that's going down the Colorado. It appeals to me; I'd like to take it. The rest of the firm is dead set against it, though."

"You haven't made a deal yet?"

"No——"

"Good!" Moran exclaimed. "I think I've got something just as interesting that will be more in your line. I suppose you know we're hauling the Silk Express across the mountains from Ogden to Denver?"

"I've heard you were. You haven't had any trouble?"

"No—and I don't want to have any. She's been running blind, stopping only for water. Pat always has armed guards aboard. But I don't mind telling you I'm in a sweat from the minute we pick her up until we turn her over in Denver. Only the chief dispatcher's office and a few top men know when she's coming through, but I don't care how closely you guard a secret like that, there's bound to be leaks. I've been a railroad man long enough to know it. Raw silk runs into money, Rainbow. Six, seven, sometimes eight cars. It don't miss the million-dollar mark by much. I know if anyone was interested they could spot the train in the yards at Ogden and telegraph ahead."

"I don't believe you have very much to worry about,"

Rainbow declared. "Silk is bulky. You can't stuff it into a gunny sack and make off with it. I don't know how many years these silk expresses have been going East. Three or four roads have hauled them and never had any trouble. I never heard that any attempt had been made to stick one up."

"That's a record I want to see continued," Moran said with a nervous chuckle. "Take a look at that map. Get west of here ten miles and you've got some mighty lonely country ahead of you all the way across Green River and through the Uintas. I get the shivers when I remember what it used to be. It was the worst outlaw-infested corner of the United States. Brown's Park, old Vernal—and all the way down to Moab and Robbers' Roost in the land of the yellow bluffs!"

"Shucks, Tom," Grumpy scoffed, "yo're goin' back to the days of the Wild Bunch and the Hole-in-the-Wall gang. Them old-timers was all cleaned out or killed off."

"I'm not so sure a new crowd hasn't grown up to take their place," Moran said soberly.

Pat Garner had come in while Moran was talking. "That's right!" he declared. "There must be a score of men with records on the loose over there. I don't have to tell you boys that it's still a lawless country. In the last six months I've seen men like Wild Bill Williams, Ben Ruby, and Blue Morgan come out of the Canyon City pen and disappear in a day or two. It's my opinion they lost no time in heading back for their stamping ground around old Fort Duchesne, or somewhere across the line in Utah."

"Where's all this leading to?" asked Rainbow. "Where do we fit into it?"

"I want you to drift through that country on both sides of the river and get a line on who's around," Moran replied. "If it takes you a month, all right. The information will be worth what it costs."

"It sounds all right to me," Grumpy spoke up as he saw his partner start to shake his head. He glared at Rainbow wrathfully. "What do you find wrong with it?"

19

"Not a thing," Rainbow replied. "I'd like it fine. But I'm going to say no."

"If it's a matter of money——" Moran picked up.

"Money hasn't anything to do with it, Tom. If you were in a spot and needed help you know what my answer would be, but if it isn't anything more serious than this I wish you'd get someone else. I want to have a fling at that Colorado River expedition. I can't tell you why; I've just got a funny feeling about it."

"By gravy, I got a feelin' about it too!' 'Grumpy exploded. "If you go, you go alone!"

If he stopped abruptly it was only because a clerk from the chief dispatcher's office ran in with a sheet of yellow tissue for Moran. The latter sucked in his breath sharply as he read the brief message. His smothered curse said that the news was bad.

"What is it, Tom?" Pat Garner demanded anxiously.

"A freight train piled up two miles west of Split Mountain! Track blocked! Engine and a couple cars in the ditch!" Moran grabbed the speaking tube that connected him with the division superintendent's office downstairs. "Matt!" he barked. "One-nineteen is in the ditch west of Split Mountain! Get a crew and wrecker on the way! That track's got to be cleared in a hurry! Let that stuff slide down into the canyon if you have to, and to the devil with it! I'll be down in a minute!"

The chief dispatcher himself ran in now, his face white with excitement. "Mr. Moran, that freight was wrecked! Logs had been piled on the track! I've got the special laid out on the siding in Mormon Valley with a burned-out bearing. One-nineteen was running on her time. Do you realize that but for that burned-out bearing the Silk Express would——"

"Jumpin' Jehoshaphat!" Moran cried. "So that's what they were after! I told you, Ripley."

Wait a minute, Tom!" Rainbow caught the railroad man by the arm as he grabbed his hat and started for the door.

20

"If that offer is still open we're taking it. But we're here without horses or saddles or any kind of an outfit——"

"Pat, see that they get what they need!" Moran ordered. "Have their horses put aboard the wrecker. You'll have to step on it! We'll be pulling out in twenty minutes!" He ran to the stairs. "I'll see you on the train, boys!" he called back.

"Waal, Rainbow, you finally came to yore senses," Grumpy growled. "Though a mountain had to fall on you first!"

Rainbow faced him with a sober countenance. "Grumpy, make no mistake about it; we're asking for cards in the biggest game we ever sat in. All the chips will be down before we're through with this business."

Half an hour later they were tearing through the night aboard the hastily assembled wrecking train. Doctors and a nurse had been recruited. A later wire had advised Moran that the fireman of the wrecked train had been killed; others of the crew were badly injured.

"I'd be careful not to say anything about the Silk Express in anything I gave out to the newspapers," Rainbow advised as he sat with Grumpy, Moran, and Garner in the swaying caboose. "Just put this job down as the work of someone who has a grudge against the railroad."

Moran nodded. "I don't intend to give out anything about the Silk Express for several reasons. This story of yours will do. Not that it will fool the gang that tried to knock her off."

"We don't want them to be fooled," said Rainbow. "They'll know we're not being fooled either. It'll give them something to think about, and they'll wonder what we're up to."

"We certainly don't want this to happen again," the gray-haired Moran muttered grimly.

"That's what Rainbow is tellin' you, Tom," Grumpy put in. "There ain't no way of slowin' up a bunch of crooks like lettin' 'em know yo're jest as smart—or a little smarter—than they are. There must've been a big bunch of 'em in on this job for 'em to figger they could git away with any quantity of stuff. I ain't no fortuneteller, but if Blue Morgan has

21

been seen anywhere between the Uintas and the San Rafael Swell, he gits my vote. I know that wolf. He don't play 'less he's head man."

In another hour the train was skirting the deep gorge of the Yampa River. A series of tunnels brought it to the Rocky Mountain Shortline's new steel bridge across the Green. Here at the head of Missionary Run the towering, sheer walls of Lodore to the north and Spirit Canyon to the south fell away until the distance between the rim and the surface of the river was barely a hundred feet. The four men stepped out on the rear platform as the train rolled across the bridge. Grumpy made a wry face as he gazed at the reddish-brown flood sweeping along beneath him.

"We're danged well done with that," he muttered.

Rainbow let it pass without comment. But there was a question in his mind, despite his tight-lipped silence. "I hope Grumpy's right," he thought. "But I wonder."

The railroad maintained a tiny office at the western approach to the bridge. The man stationed there was a combination telegrapher and watchman. The messages Moran had received had come from here. The train slowed now.

"Hey, Charlie!" called Moran as he saw the operator running alongside the cars looking for him. "You found out anything?" .

"The wire's dead west of here!" the man shouted. "Went out as I was trying to get through to the sheriff in Vernal!"

"Cut, eh?"

"Yeah! Hours ago!"

"Listen," Rainbow broke in as the train ground to a stop. "Put us off here, Tom. We're only a few miles from the wreck. We can find the break, and if you'll give me a set of leg irons and a pair of pliers I'll repair it. I want to see where the cut was made. It may tell us which way that bunch went."

"All right!" Moran agreed. "Get their horses off, Pat!"

Grumpy shifted his guns to a handier position as the train pulled away and left him and his partner on the right-of-
22

way. "What makes you think they cut the wire between the river and Split Mountain, Rainbow?" he asked.

"Only because they knew their trail would be picked up and they had to break it. I can't think of a better place for that than the Painted Bluffs. That would have sent them this way."

The little man had no fault to find with this logic. Of necessity they had to follow the roadbed. It kept them out in the open where they were easy targets. Grumpy ranged ahead, grimly alert, giving his whole attention to every rock and clump of sagebrush that might conceal a lurking enemy and leaving it to Rainbow to find the break in the wire.

Though they were forced to move slowly, they had put a good eight miles behind them, and Split Mountain was looming up through the pre-dawn grayness when Rainbow's signal announced that he had found the cut. Grumpy swung back to him quickly.

"Waal, looks like you was right!" the gnarled one declared. "Must've been quite a bunch of 'em here. The sage is all tramped down off there to the left. Reckon we can look for 'em in the Painted Bluffs, jest as you said."

"You know we won't find them." Rainbow's gaze lifted to the broken country to the south. "Only a bunch of greenhorns at this game would think of sticking together. If they try it we can forget about Blue Morgan. He's too smart for that. But we'll repair this line and then try to follow their trail."

The light was growing stronger with every passing second. By the time Rainbow climbed down the pole, the repairs finished, the sun was edging up over the horizon. There was still enough moisture in the air to keep the trail ahead of them sharp enough to be followed easily. It led steadily upward to a hard, flinty plateau. They were within a few hundred yards of it when Rainbow flung up a hand and called a halt.

"Take a look at that," he said. "They could have gone on a few minutes until they hit the hardpan and then faded away without our knowing what had become of them. But they parted company here so that a man couldn't miss what they were up to."

"Scattered like a covey of quail!" Grumpy said testily. "Better'n a dozen of 'em, and every last one of the lizards has pulled off by hisself!"

"We can turn back," Rainbow advised. "No use in looking any farther. They're back where they started from by now and telling themselves how smart they are."

"This *was* purty smart," Grumpy averred. "Jest the sort of trick Morgan used to pull when he was hoistin' banks up in Wyomin'."

Rainbow was turning his horse when he caught sight of the lid of a pasteboard box that had been carelessly tossed aside. He rode over and picked it up, and a few moments later located the bottom section of the box. It looked so new that he was sure it had not been there long. He read the printed label on the end of the box: Size 40—Pattern S P 23—Wasatch Woolen Mills, Provo, Utah.

"Shirt box," he told Grumpy. Both were familiar with the heavy woolen shirts turned out by the Wasatch Mills.

"What do you suppose it's doin' up here?" the little man asked.

"I reckon we'll have the answer to that when we see those wrecked freight cars. Chances are there was a shipment of woolen goods on that train, and one of these gents helped himself to a shirt." Rainbow broke off the part of the box on which the label was pasted and placed it in his wallet.

"I'm 'fraid that won't git you very far," Grumpy muttered. "Nine out of ten stores in this country handle them Wasatch shirts."

"I know. That's why this box was thrown away here. It didn't seem to mean anything. The mills change their patterns every few months, though. This may not be worth anything, but I'll take the label along."

When they arrived at the scene of the wreck they found

the Uinta County sheriff there with several deputies. The track had been cleared and repaired. The freight engine still lay on its side. The work crew had hold of it with a heavy steel crane and finally got it up so that it settled down on its trucks. Smashed boxes of goods lay scattered around. An assortment of woolen shirts and underwear had spilled out of a packing case, leaving no doubt that Rainbow's surmise had been correct. He and Grumpy spoke with the sheriff and his men for a minute and then went off in search of Moran, convinced that further conversation with these badge toters was a waste of time.

"They're jest over here seein' the sights," the little one rasped. "They won't be any help to us."

Rainbow nodded. "We'll play our own hand. Come on!"

"Just a second, boys," Moran called out on catching sight of them. He had been working as hard as any of his men. "We've got everything clear here. There's a siding about three miles west of the mountain. I'm going to have the wrecker push this stuff back to it so the special can come through. I'll be with you as soon as I give the orders."

He was gone only a few minutes, bringing Garner with him when he returned. The partners had very little to tell them.

"This may be a long trail, Tom," Rainbow warned. "It's dead sure to be a mean one. You won't make it any easier by trying to keep in touch with us."

"Go ahead; you're on your own," Moran told him. "Pat and I will keep out of your way." He took out one of his cards and scrawled a few words on the back of it. "Here, take this. Our agents and conductors will honor it if you happen to need them for any reason." He shook hands with them hurriedly as the engineer gave a warning toot of the whistle. "Luck to you! I know you'll come up with something!"

Grumpy recalled that optimistic parting with caustic misgiving as he rolled into his blankets one evening a week

25

later, down on the Duchesne Fork of the Uinta River. He and Rainbow had covered a lot of territory and knew no more than when they had headed south from the railroad.

"I'm shore glad you told Moran not to try to keep a finger on us," he said moodily. "Reckon if he knew how we'd fallen down on the job so far he'd be wonderin' if he made a mistake in hirin' us."

Rainbow smiled. "I guess not. We've kept on the move pretty well."

"Huh! I'll say we have!" the gnarled little man snorted. "My hunkers is sore from tryin' to find a soft spot in a saddle that don't fit me! When are we gittin' our own gear?"

"We'll start swinging back north in the morning and work out the country close to the river. If something doesn't stop us before we get there we can go over Ute Pass to Black Forks and out to the ranch."

Rainbow kicked the fire out. Caution was strong in him tonight. He knew their presence in this wild, sparsely settled country had been noted, and that a whisper had run ahead of them on some invisible grapevine telegraph. They had seen some familiar faces and talked with men whose records were bad. There had been others, ranchers and merchants of proven integrity, but they had proven as uncommunicative as those who were open to suspicion. They had shaken their heads and disclaimed any knowledge of such men as Blue Morgan, Ben Ruby, and Wild Bill Williams.

It was as though a sinister shadow lay on the land—something that could be felt if not seen. Rainbow lay there thinking it over long after Grumpy was slumbering soundly. More than once he had seen an organized gang of desperadoes terrorize a range. He could find no better explanation for the present situation. The violence and rash of brutal killings that invariably resulted from such a state of affairs had not yet broken out here. What tomorrow might bring was another story.

They had picketed their horses out on the little flat in.

which they were camped. Rainbow was giving them a last
glance before closing his eyes when he noticed that the animals had their heads up. It caught his immediate attention.
The moon was low and the dense willow brakes along the
twisting stream held the little flat in shadow. The horses'
attention was sharply fixed on the trees now.

"Grumpy!" Rainbow whispered. "Wake up! We've got
company!"

The little man sat up, blinking his eyes. "Where?" he demanded, reaching for his rifle.

"Over in the willows. Sit tight a second."

As they waited, tension building up in them, something
sailed through the air and fell at Ripley's feet. It was close
enough for him to see that it was a rock. A piece of paper
was bound around it. In a patch of filtering moonlight he
read the brief message.

Look Fer Blue At Ute Crossin'

"Come on!" Rainbow jerked out tensely. "We're going
to have a look at the gent who delivered this! Come up in
back of him! I'll go this way!"

They had not taken three steps before a crashing in the
willows warned them that their visitor did not intend to be
trapped there. Rainbow tried to turn him back toward Grumpy,
but the man was too quick for him. A few seconds later a
shadowy figure darted across an opening in the brush, evidently with the intention of reaching his horse. A warning
shot failed to stop him, and he reached the protection of a
shallow gulch. When Rainbow tried to close in, the other's
gun flamed red, and he wasn't fooling.

With the slugs whining about his ears like angry hornets,
Ripley did not stand on ceremony. Lowering his head, he
made a low, flying dive for the first convenient boulder. Before he could fire a shot, a wild shriek from Grumpy stopped
him. The little fighting wildcat had reached the top of the
gulch in back of his man. Splitting the night wide open with

his bloodcurdling war cry, he came crashing down on the surprised foe with the bone-crushing force of a battering-ram. The man's gun went flying, and when he slowly crawled to his feet Grumpy had him covered. With recognition, the little one's voice rose in another shrill cry.

"Why, you dirty ole beef-stealin' son of a skunk!" he screeched. "What's the meanin' of you throwin' lead at us? Rainbow, look what I got here! It's old Yampa Jackson!"

"It ain't no one else," Rainbow agreed as his eyes fell on the old man.

"Now wait a minute, boys!" Yampa protested before they could say more. "I didn't mean you no harm. I jest didn't want you to know who brought you that message. Blue will fill me full of holes if he finds out."

"He won't find out from us," Rainbow's tone had a grim edge. "Where do you figure in this? I thought you'd settled down to respectable living."

"I have," the snag-toothed old reprobate insisted.

"I been runnin' my saloon at Ute Crossin' fer two years and mindin' my knittin'. Of course I been sellin' a little likker to some of them reservation Utes and mebbe been a mite free with the nice fat yearlin's that drift down the crick ever onct in a while. But I ain't busted out like I used to. 'Bout four weeks ago Blue walks in one mornin' and slaps fifty dollars down on the bar an' tells me the place is his; that I kin git my belongin's an' drift, an' be damn thankful he's so generous."

The old man licked his ragged mustache, and in the moonlight his eyes were wells of hate.

"He had Wild Bill an' Ruby and Chink Johnson with him," he went on. "I told Jenny—she's my squaw—to roll the blankets, that we was movin'." He waggled his head gravely. "I been keepin' my mouth shut, but I aim to git even."

"Yampa, was Blue mixed up in wrecking that train at Split Mountain?"

The old man's rheumy eyes narrowed at the question. "I wouldn't know, Rainbow——"

"You know, but you won't say. Is that it?"

Yampa Jackson rubbed his chin thoughtfully for a moment. "Boys, you know my principles. I don't do any tongue-waggin' about what's cookin' in the other feller's pot."

"All right," Rainbow told him. "Find your horse and get out of here."

In a few minutes they heard him riding away. They listened until the night was still again.

"You find friends in strange places in this business of ours," Rainbow murmured.

"Good Christopher!" Grumpy burst out. "You ain't swallerin' that story, are you? That thievin' ole booger would sell out St. Peter for a ten-cent piece! If this ain't a trap I'm loco!"

"I don't know," Rainbow admitted soberly, "but we're gettin out of here right now."

Chapter Four

WE GOIN' TO RIDE the rest of this night?" Grumpy demanded. "We must've come fifteen miles. I reckon if there was anyone tailin' us we lost 'em a long way back."

"We've come far enough," Rainbow informed him. "Cut down the slope to that clump of aspens and we'll pull the saddles off these horses and try to get a little sleep. I'm going in to Vernal in the morning and see if there's an answer to the letter I sent the Wasatch Woolen Mills. That'll leave us the rest of the day to get over the divide above Ute Crossing."

Rainbow found a reply to his letter awaiting him in Vernal. He read it with evident satisfaction.

"No need to ask if the news is up to yore expectations," his partner observed dryly. "That pussy cat grin is answer enough."

"The number I sent them is a new one, they say," Rainbow told him. "Some shipments have gone out, but none locally. They've sent along a sample of the material. Here it is!"

Grumpy had a look at it. "Kind o' like one of them Scotch plaids. They're all pretty much the same to me."

"No two of 'em are alike," Rainbow told him. "I'll explain that to you some day. It's quite a story."

. Riding past a saloon as they were leaving town, they saw a dark-faced man in worn overalls and a sweat-stained Stetson eyeing them curiously. Rainbow glanced back to see him disappearing into the barroom with undue haste.

"That tough-looking gent will be out the back door and heading for his horse in a minute," he told Grumpy. "He's going to tail us, unless I miss my guess."

"Suppose we shake him off right now," Grumpy suggested. "These broncs are fresh. Throw the steel into 'em!"

They were followed, but in the wild, broken country to the north it was easy to discourage pursuit. After losing sight of the lone rider they saw no one for the rest of the morning. By early afternoon they were on Ute Creek. Keeping to the rim of the shallow canyon through which it flowed eventually brought them within sight of the Crossing. By that time the afternoon was half gone.

"I don't know what's down there. It looks peaceful enough, but we shore better size it up purty careful before we go bustin' in." Grumpy gave the horse shed in back of the unpainted, weather-beaten dive a close scrutiny. The saloon boards covering its broken windows, the shed, and a barn that tilted so crazily on its rotten underpinning that it promised to collapse at any moment were the only buildings in Ute Crossing. "Four, five broncs tethered in the shed," he announced.

Rainbow nodded. "Business must be good."

They had reconnoitered the place for half an hour when a man came to the door and tossed out a pailful of slops. He was too far away for them to say who he was. But Rainbow had reached a decision.

"It'd be foolish to try to walk in and surprise them," he said. "Our best bet is to cut over to the road and ride up as though we had a right to. If Blue's down there, there won't be any gunplay! He knows we'd do something about that. He also knows we haven't any evidence against him. If he isn't there look out for trouble!"

"A bushel of it, I reckon!" Grumpy scratched his head thoughtfully for a moment. "It's yore opinion that Yampa Jackson told us a reasonably straight story, eh?"

"No, this may be a jackpot. Whatever it is we've got to crack it. Well, if you're ready we'll go."

A few minutes after they reached the road they came in sight of the saloon. They took it for granted that they were seen. Jogging up to the open door, they stepped down from their saddles and walked in. They found five men, counting the bartender, in the room. The way they had arranged themselves—a man at either end of the bar, one at a table to the rear, and the fourth occupying a tilted chair by the window—said plainly enough that they had not been surprised.

"Well, old home week!" Rainbow laughed. The men Yampa had mentioned were all present, save Blue himself.

A strained silence greeted the sally. The partners walked up to the bar and Ripley tossed a silver dollar on the counter. "Rye," he said.

Grumpy swung around carelessly, his back to the bar, ready for whatever was to come.

The bartender was slow in setting out a bottle and glasses. Rainbow's attention was nicely divided between him and the reflection in the cracked backbar mirror of the moonfaced man who sprawled in the chair by the window, a tough, thickskulled young desperado who answered to the name of Chink Johnson. He had a record a yard long and had done time in three or four states. Ripley was particularly interested in the shirt Chink was wearing. It was spotted and grease-stained, but it was new, and Rainbow told himself if it had

31

not been cut from the same goods as the sample he had received that morning his eyes were tricking him.

"Took you a long while to get around." A voice broke up the weighted quiet of the room. "I figured you gents would be lookin' me up."

Out of the corner of his eye Rainbow saw Blue Morgan filling the doorway that led to the back room. It was Blue's boast that he had a great sense of humor. There was a grin on his dark face now, but his eyes were not smiling. He came up in back of the bar and poured himself a drink with studied deliberation. "What's on your mind?" He spoke with the faintest suggestion of a lisp. Years of trying to hide the affliction had resulted in his speaking with the barest possible movement of his lips. It made a mouth that had never been touched with mercy or pity doubly forbidding.

"Nothing in particular," Rainbow returned casually. "Yampa around?"

Grumpy heard the question without raising an eyebrow, but he wondered at Rainbow's asking it.

"Not any more," answered Blue. "I'm runnin' this joint."

"So?" Ripley jerked his head to indicate the customers. "Looks as though business was improving. That homemade white mule old Yampa used to cook up wasn't anything to make a man come back twice."

They were only fencing. It didn't satisfy Morgan.

"Any reason why the boys shouldn't drop in?" he demanded more pointedly.

"Not at all. They've got to have some place to do their homework."

Blue's eyes took on a harder glint, but he laughed. "You're quite a joker, Ripley! I hear you're working for the railroad."

He realized that he had said almost too much even before Grumpy growled: "News shore gits around in a hurry, don't it? Ask him where he got his information, Rainbow!"

"It's no secret," his partner countered. He knew what he wanted, and he didn't propose to let the situation get away from him. "We're trying to find out who wrecked that freight

32

over at Split Mountain, Morgan. It wasn't robbery. The company figured someone was squaring a grudge."

"So they say," Blue muttered. Something in his eyes said he was not being fooled.

"I aim to find out what old Yampa knows about it," Rainbow persisted. "He used to do a lot of blowin' off about getting even with the Shortline because they wouldn't recognize his title to that range he'd been squatting on over at Ashley."

This was sheer invention, but it was good enough. Chink Johnson and the others relaxed. Even Blue seemed to find possibilities in the idea.

"That old bag of bones is half cracked," he declared. "No tellin' what he'd do. He must be somewhere around the Agency."

"Thanks," Rainbow murmured. "We'll be heading that way."

With a word to Grumpy he started out.

"Drop in again some time," Blue invited as the partners were riding away.

"We will," Rainbow called back.

Grumpy heaved a heavy sigh of relief when they had put the shoulder of the first mountain between themselves and Ute Crossing. "The ole ticker was standin' still there for a minute or two," he declared. "That was a fine cock-and-bull story about Yampa Jackson bein' mixed up in this. But they swallered it. Reckon they figger we're jest a pair of half-wits."

"We'll have to convince 'em of it," Rainbow said, grinning. "The best way to do it is to slap Yampa into jail and hold him on suspicion for a few weeks. He won't mind; he'll feel right to home. Did you get a good look at the shirt Chink was wearing?"

"Did I?" the little man grunted. "Reckon we know where it came from!"

Ripley nodded. "We may be mistaken, but it wouldn't seem so."

33

Grumpy glared at him disgustedly. "Good gravy! You know they're the bunch that wrecked that train!"

"No doubt about it, but we're a long way from proving it."

They did not overlook the chance that Morgan would have one of his men trailing them. Accordingly, when they reached the fork in the road that led to the Uinta Agency, they turned off and made a bluff at riding in, though they knew Yampa was certainly not there. From a point of vantage they watched the road north for an hour. They were not far from the line now, and it was their intention to go over Ute Pass and on to Black Forks that evening. Deciding finally that it was safe to put in an appearance, even though the Agency road was being watched, they started to climb into their saddles only to be stopped by the sight of two riders coming up from the direction of the Crossing. The two horsemen were moving right along.

"Huh!" Grumpy jerked out. "It's Blue and Chink Johnson! We'll wish we'd gone on to the Agency if they turn up this way!"

"They're moving too fast to be looking for us," argued Rainbow. "They're going over the pass too."

Morgan and Johnson reined up sharply, however, as they reached the forks. A glance at the tracks in the dust seemed to satisfy them, and they soon disappeared to the north.

"Can't be too careful with them gents," Grumpy remarked. "Guess we kin be movin' now."

Evening was closing down by the time they rode into Black Forks. The increased activity on the banks of the river and double the number of tents they had last observed there told them Professor Hammersley and his party had arrived from the East.

"I suppose Hammersley wonders where we are," Rainbow remarked. "I wrote him he'd find us here."

"It'll be a pleasure to tell him we're doin' somethin' else," piped up Grumpy. "We kin ride down after we git a line on what Morgan's doin' here."

34

At the hotel the clerk told them Professor Hammersley had been inquiring about them. Rainbow registered, and he was surprised to see Blue Morgan's signature on the line above his own. "We'll have Room 5 again if it's just the same to you," he told the boy.

Cold water and a clean shave sharpened the edge of their appetites, and they were about to go down to supper when they heard someone enter the room next door. Rainbow put his ear to the wall and listened until he was convinced that their neighbor was alone.

"What was the idee of that?" asked Grumpy.

Rainbow smiled. "Do you know who we've got next door?"

"No."

"Blue. That's why I asked for this room."

After they had eaten they took a turn up and down the street. A light burned in Morgan's room and the shade was down.

"Looks like he was expectin' company," Grumpy observed. "Mebbe we better—— Say, what's eatin' you?" he said sharply as Rainbow caught him by the arm and pulled him back when he would have crossed the street. The other had just noticed Chink Johnson leaning against the hitch rack of the saloon opposite. Chink's attitude was not that of a man who had ridden into town and was only killing time. His attention was fixed on the newspaper office next door, inside of which the partners could see Ed Burgess, the editor, talking to a rocky-faced man in a belted corduroy coat of military cut.

When the stranger came out Chink stepped up to him and handed him a note. The man took it and continued up the street. Rainbow and Grumpy saw him stop in front of the lighted windows of the general store and read the message. Surprise and rage chased each other across his hard face.

"Whatever it is, he don't like it," Grumpy muttered. "Acts as though it smacked him straight between the eyes."

The man started to tear up the note, then crammed it in

his pocket. After a moment's hesitation he swung around on his heels and made directly for the hotel.

"Come on!" Rainbow got out quickly. "This may be the party Blue's waiting to see. We'll get there ahead of him!"

A few seconds after they reached their room they heard a loud knock at Morgan's door and then Blue saying: "It's open! Walk in!"

The stranger entered, slamming the door behind him.

"It's been a long time, Brant, since our trails crossed. Take a chair." Morgan's tone belied the hospitality he offered.

"No, we'll make this short!" was the hostile answer.

"The shorter the better," Blue said with flinty inflection. "We can discuss our business in a hurry and without blattin' it out for the rest of the hotel to hear. The walls in this dump are damned thin."

Brant took the hint. They talked for four or five minutes, and neither Rainbow nor Grumpy could catch what they were saying. Finally Morgan burst out angrily: "Don't try to fill me full of anythin' like that! This guy Hammersley and his bunch don't mean a damned thing to me! They look crazy enough to risk their necks tryin' to find mineral deposits down the canyons. But not you, Brant! You got somethin' else up your sleeve!"

"I'm being well paid for my services," Samson Brant said flatly. "Hammersley's got a lot of money. Why shouldn't I take the good pickings?"

"Don't kid me!" Morgan rapped out fiercely. "I know what your game is, and I'm tellin' you to forget it!"

Brant met the challenge with a contemptuous laugh. "I didn't think you'd have the brass to put anything up to me like that! You get in my way and you'll get hurt!"

"You've had your warnin'!" Blue flung at him. "I've sized up the crowd you've got here with you an' I can match 'em, man for man!"

"You fool!" Anger and contempt strove for mastery in Brant. With a curse he flung himself out of the room. Rain-

36

bow and Grumpy could hear him clumping down the stairs. In about five minutes Blue Morgan departed.

"Waal, what do you make of that?" Grumpy demanded excitedly. "This Brant must be Hammersley's right-hand man. What's this game Blue says he's wise to? And what is there down them canyons that he don't want Brant to git his hands on? Is he figgerin' to kidnap them perfessors or rob 'em blind? Or what the dang-blasted answer is there to this riddle?"

Rainbow had no immediate answer. "What's the point in guessing?" he inquired flatly. "All I can tell you now is that I wasn't saying more than I meant when I told you we were taking cards in the biggest game of our lives. For the present we'll keep our mouths shut and saw wood. Come on! We're going to see Professor Hammersley!"

Chapter Five

*G*ETTING THEIR HORSES, the partners rode down to the camp. Brant's men had made a bonfire of driftwood. Enjoying its warmth, the members of the expedition sat around discussing their plans for the trip. Some of them were still seated at the long table where they had had supper.

When Rainbow and Grumpy were within a hundred yards of the fire they were stopped in quite the same manner as on their previous visit. Again it was Ginger Revell who confronted them. When he saw who they were he lost some of his surliness.

"I guess yo're expected," he said. "The perfessor's over there at the table." He indicated the direction with his rifle and they rode on.

"They're a queer-lookin' lot," Grumpy muttered under his breath, his glance traveling from Saburo Itchi to Dr. Johan Borelius, the well-known geologist from Sweden, and on to Anne Wattress, the landscape painter. "A woman in breeches, an' puffin' a cigarette! Blue had 'em sized up right!"

Rainbow's attention was focused on the dark-haired girl who turned to greet them. "This must be Rainbow Ripley and his partner!" he heard her tell the others.

If Rainbow failed to catch the appraising glance that Itchi and Hammersley gave him, Samson Brant did not. The three were seated together at the end of the table. "Remember what I told you in New York," Brant reminded them under his breath. "They're as shrewd as they look!"

"I was disappointed not to find you here when we arrived," the professor told the partners. He introduced them to the others. "You're just in time; we expect to leave in the morning. Everything is in readiness. After tonight the stars will be our tent."

For a time the conversation was general. Rainbow found himself cataloging these people and trying to fit them into a pattern. Borelius, Thursby, a photographer, and little Ulysses S. Potts, the eminent zoologist, were easily disposed of. Karen Thane and Miss Wattress were patently above suspicion. Professionally, the undertaking promised opportunities as interesting to them as anything Borelius or Dr. Potts hoped to find. If Rainbow did not dismiss young Jim Darwin, the ethnologist, with the others it was only because he felt that Darwin's real interest in the expedition was Professor Hammersley's ward, Karen Thane. Samson Brant he knew to be a crook. Hammersley himself and the wooden-faced Itchi raised a long series of questions in his mind, however, and he refused to accept them as just a pair of guileless and innocent scientific adventurers.

"Let us step into my tent," the professor suggested when the fire had burned down and Miss Wattress and several others had said good night. "We will find it warmer inside; I have a small primus stove. We will miss such little conveniences. I'm afraid. Unfortunately we must leave all this camping equipment behind."

Itchi held up the tent flap. Rainbow was about to follow the others when Karen Thane offered him her hand and said good night.

"I'm so glad you are going with us," she said sincerely. "I'm sure we shall all feel safer. I know I shall."

Rainbow knew a moment's deep regret at having to tell her that Grumpy and he would not be accompanying them. He was about to speak when young Darwin inserted himself into the situation. He seemed to resent the girl's friendliness and interest in Ripley.

"I didn't know you had any misgivings about the trip, Karen," he remarked contentiously. "You know I will look out for you. A boat may be swamped, but Mr. Ripley could hardly prevent that. We'll be wearing cork life jackets, so the worst you have to fear is a wetting."

Darwin was a clear-eyed youngster, with the body of an athlete. Several years of field work in the Southwest had tanned his skin a healthy brown. Rainbow did not hold the man's resolve to elect himself Karen Thane's protector against him. In fact, it was a privilege he himself would have relished. This eager, dark-eyed girl stirred him deeply. No other reason prompted him to put off telling her that he was not going along.

"I'll see you in the morning," he promised. "We'll have more to say about this."

He found Grumpy and the others waiting for him inside.

"I've left it to you to tell 'em how things stand," the little fellow told his partner. His tone said definitely that they were to hear news. Itchi's face remained a perfect mask, and the only betraying sign of Hammersley's quickened interest was a faint contraction of the eyes. Samson Brant did not bother to dissemble his elation.

"It's just that circumstances have come up that make it impossible for us to accept your offer, Professor," Rainbow said. The conflicting reactions of the three men were not lost on him.

"You . . . mean you have a job?" Hammersley inquired.

"We're working for the Rocky Mountain Shortline."

It was a bombshell, and only imperturbable Saburo Itchi heard it explode without a trace of surprise.

"Is that so?" Hammersley queried. "That's very unfortunate. Very!" It was a strangely prophetic utterance, though he did not intend it as such. Unconsciously his piercing eyes began to burn with their peculiar fire at this dangerous upsetting of his plans.

"We can't blame you for taking a job like that. After all, it's steady work," Brant put in. "We'll have to get along without you." He was relieved, and his tone gave every indication of it.

Rainbow told them how he and Grumpy had been called over to Platte City by Moran. "Working for a railroad is a new experience for us," he sad. "But we owed Moran a favor. When word came in that somebody had wrecked a freight at Split Mountain we felt we had to take the job."

"Of course," Itchi murmured, moving into the breach as he saw Hammersley and Brant stiffen at this news. "It sounds very exciting." He turned to the professor. "You see, Doctor, the West is still wild. Robbery was the motive, I presume. But I do not seem to remember reading about this affair in the newspaper, Mr. Ripley. It occurred some time ago?"

"No, just a week ago yesterday. About nine o'clock in the evening."

He was deliberately supplying the Japanese with the information he felt the other secretly wanted. Hammersley and Brant had followed this apparent bit of dialogue with marked attention. Their eyes remained fixed on Saburo. The latter nodded almost imperceptibly.

Rainbow caught it and could only guess at its significance. Its effect on Brant was immediate, however. Something touched his rocky face and left it bloodless for a moment. He was in the dark as to Itchi's sources of information regarding the silk expresses, but he had satisfied himself that the Nipponese knew when they were due to come through. These questions about the time of the wreck had but one purpose, and when Itchi nodded Brant knew that the wrecking of the freight had resulted from a bungled attempt to stop a silk train.

Brant had said nothing to Hammersley about his meeting with Blue Morgan; he had not taken Blue too seriously. He was of another opinion now, and his first thought was to get down to the river and warn Revell and the rest of his hand-picked thugs to be ready for trouble.

A few minutes after Brant left the tent Professor Hammersley got to his feet, signifying that the interview was over; he had been shaken by the news and he wanted to be alone with Itchi.

"We'll say good night," Rainbow drawled. "We'll see you for a minute in the morning."

"Yeah," Grumpy echoed. It was the first word he had spoken in minutes. "Pleased to have met yuh, Perfessor and Mr. Itchi."

He was nearest the entrance. He reached out to raise the flap, and just as he did so a gun barked at the river's edge. It was followed by a second and third shot, evidently from the same weapon.

Rainbow and the little man rushed out, closely followed by Hammersley and Itchi. In a moment the whole camp was in commotion.

"Those shots came from down where the boats are tied up!" Rainbow exclaimed. He ran that way, Grumpy and the others a step behind him. They had gone only a few yards when they saw Brant standing on the bank, a smoking pistol in his hand.

"What is it, Brant?" Rainbow demanded.

"Somebody was trying to make off with our boats. I stopped him. I suppose he knew they were loaded with cameras and expensive equipment."

41

Jim Darwin ran up, a candle lantern in his hand.

"Let's have that light!" Grumpy growled. Grabbing the lantern, he and Rainbow ran ahead.

"There he is," Rainbow muttered as he caught sight of the man sprawled out grotesquely on the wet bank. "Grumpy, it's Chink Johnson!"

"An' he's deader'n a mackerel!"

Before the others arrived Ripley cut a piece out of the dead's man's shirt and slipped it into a pocket. "Let's get away from here as soon as we can," he said hurriedly. "This bird wasn't trying to steal this stuff with the idea of turning it into cash. Blue was out to stop this expedition before it ever got started."

Hammersley and three or four others reached them a moment later. With a complete absence of feeling Itchi examined the body and then raised his inscrutable eyes to Samson Brant.

"I congratulate you on your marksmanship, Mr. Brant," he murmured. From his tone he might have been discussing some interesting laboratory experiment. "Any one of your three shots would have killed him."

"Well! I must say I was not prepared for anything of this nature." Thaddeus Hammersley spoke with undiluted honesty for a change. Rainbow suspected as much. "Brant, do you know this man?"

"Never laid eyes on him before," was the prompt answer. Grumpy and Rainbow exchanged a glance.

"I can help you out," the latter volunteered. "He called himself Chink Johnson. He's run afoul of the law a number of times. I guess there won't be any question about this shooting, but the sheriff will have to be called in."

"He shall be notified at once," the professor assured him. "I hope this does not hold us up for any length of time."

"I don't know any reason why it should," said Ripley. "But I'll speak to Effingham."

He and Grumpy made their way back to their horses. They found Karen Thane waiting for them and making no attempt to conceal her alarm. The shooting had only confirmed her growing feeling that something sinister was moving under the surface close to her.

"This is a tragic beginning," she said, trying to hold her voice steady. "You see, my fears were well founded. I . . . I hope this isn't a forerunner of worse things to come."

Rainbow gazed at her with deep concern. "Miss Thane, why do you say that?"

"I . . . I don't know," Karen answered nervously. "It's just that nothing seems to be quite right. These men Mr. Brant has engaged do not inspire any confidence in me. And Uncle—Dr. Hammersley—seems so preoccupied and not like himself at all. I . . . I'm afraid for him, I couldn't say why."

"I don't believe there's any reason to be alarmed any more tonight," Rainbow said reassuringly. On the spot he made a secret decision. "You . . . wouldn't consider letting the expedition go on without you?"

"Why, no," she said. "I couldn't withdraw now! I've dreamed of a chance like this so long. It means so much to me——"

Rainbow nodded understandingly. "I figured that was the way you felt."

"There's a fine girl," Grumpy told him as they rode back to Black Forks.

"Too fine to be put up against a deal like this." Ripley's tone was grim. "I promise you I'll have something to say about this!"

The grizzled little man flicked a troubled glance at him, wondering just what the remark meant. He knew they were still only grabbing at the loose ends of this tangled web of crime and intrigue, but he was as fully convinced as Rainbow that the Hammersley Expedition held the answer to the riddle.

"Turn up the lamp," Ripley told him as they stepped into their hotel room. "We'll settle one thing in a hurry."

Placing the piece of goods that he had cut out of Chink

43

Johnson's shirt on the dresser, he laid the sample from the Wasatch Mills down beside it. The two pieces matched perfectly.

"Waal, it ain't no more than we expected," Grumpy said disparagingly. "It's evidence, but Johnson's dead. You'll find yoreself whistlin' up Windy Creek if you try to use it to pin anythin' on Morgan."

"I wasn't thinking of Blue; I wanted to be sure of this in my own mind." Rainbow placed the two pieces of cloth in an envelope and put them away for safekeeping.

Grumpy had pulled off his boots and was preparing for bed. "You goin' to turn in?" he questioned.

"Before I do I'm going downstairs and write a letter and make sure that it goes out to the ranch in the morning."

That brought the little one's head up sharply. "Why is that? I thought we was goin' out ourselves."

"Grumpy, how long should it take Hammersley to reach Brown's Park?"

"Ten days at most. There's some bad places in Red Canyon, but nuthin' to what they'll meet once they git below the park." The little man's eyes had fastened on Rainbow with sobering intensity. "Why do you ask?"

"Because we're going that far with them. I'll ask the judge to have Howie Hallett meet us there with our horses and gear."

The expected explosion did not come. Instead, Grumpy sat there on the edge of the bed, frowning at his toes and saying nothing for a minute.

"Yo're right!" he agreed at last. "We're in this now. If we're goin' to see it through we better git us some front-row seats. Between here and Brown's Park we oughta be able to bust the lid off of somethin'!"

Chapter Six

$\mathcal{J}$IM McBRIDE, who was to guide the Hammersley Expedition in the much-publicized descent of the Colorado, had gone almost unnoticed during the stay at Black Forks, but once the boats were actually moving down the river he quickly established his importance, with even Hammersley deferring to his judgment. McBride claimed that he had run the upper canyons several times.

Rainbow and Grumpy had no reason to doubt him, and by the time they reached the Flaming Gorge, two days later, they were convinced that the man knew the river. Keeping the boats strung out, so that disaster to one would not endanger the others, he skillfully avoided the treacherous Suck at the entrance to the gorge. Once inside the portal, they found themselves floating on tranquil waters. Along the eastern wall the cottonwoods were breaking into bloom. Through their yellow-green lace tier on tier of mighty red rocks reared their heads, so evenly placed it seemed a race of unknown Titans had once toiled here.

Grumpy rested on his oar, paying silent tribute to the majestic beauty of the scene unfolding about them. He turned then and spoke to Borelius, the Swede. "This is yore first good look at the Uintas. Some of them peaks climb up in the sky a ways!"

"Magnificent!" Borelius exclaimed. "Reminds me of home!"

Rainbow and Grumpy found Borelius a pleasant companion. Together with big Gass Labelle, the black-browed French Canadian whom Brant had rescued from jail, the four men comprised the crew of this boat.

Labelle had the strength of an ox. Borelius, though he was

no longer young, possessed a brawny pair of shoulders. It led Rainbow to believe that their boat was the best manned in the party. He was further convinced of it when they ran the rapids in Horseshoe Canyon without scraping an oar. The others were not so fortunate. Jim Darwin's boat struck a ledge and he was tossed into the foaming river. Grumpy and Borelius fished him out. A minute later Brant's craft swung around broadside in a swirl of white water and all but turned over. It hung there perilously, and only Jim McBride's insistence that all blankets, supplies, and instruments be kept in rubber bags and stowed away in the compartments under sealed hatches saved them from being lost.

The mishaps cost an hour, but before the afternoon was gone Horseshoe and Kingfisher had been left behind and they were well into the twenty-five-mile trough of Red Canyon. It was no longer necessary to touch the oars, except to guide the boats. The pitch of the river was steeper, the current sweeping along, pocked with treacherous boils and whirlpools. The whole appearance of the country had changed. The trees had disappeared. Not a bird was to be seen. Grim, unbroken, the canyon walls rose sheer for twenty-five hundred feet.

Glancing ahead, Rainbow could see great rocks rearing up out of the river and running together as though to make passage impossible. Even the walls of the canyon seemed to pinch suddenly, squeezing the river between them. A distant thunder reached his ears. In a few minutes its wild roar filled the canyon. All the beasts of the jungle, crying out in their wrath, could not have matched it.

"Say, that sounds bad!" Grumpy burst out. "What can you see?"

"It must be Ashley Falls!" Ripley shouted. He could glimpse now where the river, swollen by this temporary check, fought its way through the cliffs. It dropped out of sight for a few yards, but beyond it was an unbroken sheet of churning white water. Sight of it was enough to tighten his mouth. "McBride is mad if he tries to run the falls tonight!"

They were second in line in the flotilla of eleven. McBride was in the heavily laden lead boat, with Hammersley, Itchi, and two of Brant's men. Labelle, in the stern, kept his eyes fixed on the craft ahead.

"McBride, she's signaling to us now!" Labelle yelled a moment later. They saw that the guide had raised his oar and was motioning for them to make for a low, rocky bar at the base of the west wall.

" 'Bout time!" Grumpy growled. "Put some stuff on these oars!"

Pulling across the current with a will, they reached the bar ahead of the first boat. At the last moment the torrent caught them with unexpected force, and they could feel the keel grating dangerously as they dashed up on the bar. Stout as the hulls were, Rainbow knew the boats could not stand much of this. Wading into the water up to their waists, they caught the other boats as they rushed in, checking their speed. He could see that even Hammersley and the Japanese had caught the excitement of this hazardous tilting with the river. For a moment the two men seemed to forget the malign purpose of the expedition, and this coming to grips with nature in one of its wildest moods was uppermost in their minds.

Samson Brant was the last man ashore. He had just stepped out of his boat when a rifle cracked up on the rim of the canyon wall, far above. The range was almost eight hundred yards, long even for a high-powered gun. The slug found its intended mark, however. Blood spurted over Brant's face, and the impact of the bullet spun him around and flung him down on the sand.

The unseen marksman, evidently believing he had accomplished his purpose, did not fire a second time. Ginger Revell and four or five others grabbed their rifles and spattered the rim with a vicious fusillade.

"Move in nearer to the wall!" Ripley cried. "You look out for the women, Darwin!" He and Grumpy picked Brant up and carried him back to where the cliff cut in enough to make any sniping from above impossible.

Little Ulysses Potts came to take care of Brant's wound and proved himself a capable doctor. "A bloody wound," he said, "but not a serious one. He will be all right in a few minutes." He bandaged Brant's head, and a few moments after he finished the latter sat up, staring about him uncertainly as consciousness returned.

"That was a close call, Brant," Professor Hammersley said, more alarmed than he chose to admit. "I suppose we should have been expecting something like this after what happened at Black Forks." With the killing of Chink Johnson, Brant had found it advisable to give Hammersley and Itchi the details of Morgan's threat.

"You're right," Brant muttered. "I suppose this was some friend of Johnson——"

"Blue Morgan would be the name," Rainbow put in quietly. Watching the effect of his statement on the three men convinced him that Hammersley and his secretary shared Brant's knowledge of Blue.

"You may be right; I wouldn't know," Brant declared gruffly. "You're handing out a name that doesn't mean a thing to me. I——"

"Perhaps Mr. Ripley can tell us something about the gentleman." Itchi cut Brant off before he could make any damaging admission.

Rainbow nodded. "I'll be glad to." This wasn't the first time he had seen the unsmiling, carefully mannered Oriental take command of the conversation when it touched precarious ground. It confirmed his opinion that Itchi was fully as dangerous as the other two. He knew the question that was running through their minds. Having brought Blue's name up, they were asking themselves how much more he knew. "Morgan's only been out of the penitentiary several months, but he's already got together a gang of desperate, hard-riding men who carry their law on their hip," he told them. "Chink Johnson was one of them. We showed up in Black Forks when we did because we had trailed Blue and his man Johnson

48

into town that evening. We were curious to know what their business was there."

"You . . . found out?" Hammersley queried. His tone wasn't as casual as he thought.

Rainbow shrugged. "Partly," he said.

He had deliberately increased the suspicion against Grumpy and himself. The little man took him to task about it the second they were alone.

"Well, in your own words, you figured we might be able to bust the lid off of something by tagging along," Rainbow answered. "This was my way of doing it. This will thaw out something, I promise you."

He was hardly prepared for the turn it was to take, however. For obvious reasons, Utah Jim McBride ordered that no fire be lighted that evening. After eating a cold supper the members of the expedition broke up into little groups. Brant's men drew off by themselves. When Ripley looked around for Grumpy he found the crusty little man enjoying the company of Anne Wattress. The sight made Rainbow smile. "Filling her full of some tall tales," he mused.

Jim Darwin hailed Rainbow through the deepening shadows as he walked to the end of the bar.

"Sit down with us a minute, Rainbow," Darwin urged. "Karen and I want to talk to you."

Ripley was glad to oblige.

"Before we say any more," Darwin told him, "I want to take back what I said in Black Forks about our not being likely to run into any trouble. I was wrong, and I admit it. I suppose Brant was within his rights in shooting the man who was trying to steal our boats; certainly the sheriff seemed to think so. But isn't it a fact that if the dead man's friends are out for revenge that they can take pot shots at us all the way down the river?"

Rainbow shook his head. "No, this is one of the few places where it would be possible; I know that country up above.

49

Most of the cliffs are so sheer that not even a mountain sheep could get a toe hold on them."

"That's something to be thankful for," Darwin said. "You didn't foresee this sniping, of course? That couldn't have been what you had in mind that evening?"

"No," Ripley answered. Seeing the direction the conversation was taking, he was anxious to turn it. He knew they would hear from Morgan again, that Blue would make another, and possibly more successful, attempt to stop them before they had proceeded much farther. That danger was as nothing, he felt, to those that menaced the expedition from within. To say anything concerning the latter was impossible, and to mention the other could only add to Karen Thane's already deep sense of alarm. "The river seems to be our most immediate problem," he said finally. "I don't know how McBride expects to get these boats over the falls without capsizing everyone."

"I was just speaking with him," Karen said. "He thinks we will have to let them down on ropes. Uncle spent weeks designing the boats for this trip, but McBride damns them at every opportunity.

"Yeah, I've heard him." Ripley laughed. "We may be half the day getting them over."

"So he says, but I gather it's his secret opinion that we'll be lucky to get them over at all." Karen pretended to dismiss it lightly, but Rainbow saw her wince as she listened to the wild roar of the falls. "It's like Niagara beating in your ears," she said in a very small voice.

"These things always seem worse at night," Darwin told her reassuringly. "The mishaps we've had so far always beset an expedition when it's starting out. Ashley Falls won't stop us. The experiences we are having here will toughen us up for what we have ahead of us . . . down in Lodore and Desolation."

"Of course, Jim," she murmured. She was silent for a moment, and then without warning she said: "Rainbow, why did you change your mind about coming with us at the last moment, after you had said it would be impossible? Was it because you feared an attempt would be made to stop us from making the descent?"

"Why, no," Rainbow answered without hesitation, though the question had taken him by surprise. It was the second time in a few minutes that he had felt his hand being forced. He gave Karen a disarming smile. "I thought I might kill two birds with one stone. I was not only interested in the expedition, but I wanted to give Blue Morgan the idea that I wasn't watching him too closely. The Rocky Mountain Shortline would feel easier if Morgan were back in jail."

This was a long way around the bush, but it seemed to satisfy Karen. Hammersley, the Japanese, and Brant also had their heads together over this question of the sudden change of mind by Rainbow and Grumpy and had arrived at a very different answer.

The three men had drawn off to themselves where they could talk without any chance of being overheard. They were agreed that the partners were not only acutely suspicious but possibly were aware of their plans.

"I warned you in New York that Ripley and Gibbs were poison; but you wouldn't listen to me!" Brant was a fearsome figure in his wrath. "Even when you found that they were working for the Rocky Mountain Shortline you refused to see it my way!" He glared at Hammersley contemptuously. "I know you figure the brains are all on your side. If the two of you are that bright, maybe you can tell me why Ripley flung Morgan's name in our teeth tonight."

"Obviously he hoped to surprise us into some damaging admission," Itchi answered him. "You all but permitted him to succeed." Without raising his voice he silenced Brant. "He and his partner were in Black Forks the night you met Morgan at the hotel. However little they know about what was said at that meeting, it is too much. I suspect they know all about it."

Brant wondered, too, though he protested vehemently that it was impossible.

"Your discretion has never impressed me," Hammersley rebuked him. "Keeping the matter back until circumstances compelled you to speak is only further proof of your stupidity. Ripley pretended to accept our explanation of the attempt to steal the boats. That deception should be enough in itself to tell us where we stand. Now he is so sure of himself that he deliberately arouses our suspicions."

"What are we going to do about it?" Brant growled. "That's all I want to know from you. We'll be in Brown's Park in three or four days. If we let that pair ride off about their business it'll be just the same as putting a gun to our heads!"

"They'll never see Brown's Park." The professor's eyes burned in the darkness. "Itchi and I will attend to that. In formulating our plans we recognized that the need for drastic action might arise."

"Definitely," the Nipponese murmured grimly.

In the morning Professor Hammersley and McBride succeeded in climbing up the wall for a distance of several hundred feet, from which point of vantage they made a careful study of the falls. On rejoining the others Hammersley announced that he was confident they could make this drop without any great danger.

"There's fast, bad water just below the falls," McBride warned. The current'll throw you acrost to the right. You'll be in trouble if you smash into that ledge."

The professor now announced that he was making some changes in the personnel of the various boats, in order that the strength of the crews might be more evenly matched. There was grumbling at this from the members of the expedition who had assigned themselves to one craft or another with more regard for pleasant companionship than any measuring of strength with the oars.

It was a move that won Rainbow's approval, however, especially when he saw Borelius put in with Karen. His enthusiasm dimmed when Saburo Itchi was assigned to the doctor's former place. Grumpy didn't like it either.

"That's givin' us the worst pick in the bunch," the little one grumbled. "It'll be an end to any loose talk in this boat."

"At least he'll hold up his end with the oars," Rainbow said. "These Japs are tireless."

A disparaging grunt was Grumpy's answer. "They got some trick wrestlin' holts. That's about all, I reckon. But I wouldn't care if he had the strength of the devil. I don't like the way that slant-eyed drink of ice water shows his teeth!"

Brant had selected four of his most experienced men to handle the ropes. They were to remain above the falls until the other boats were down. It then would be necessary for them to go over and trust to luck to see them through. But by that time there would be plenty of help below to go to their rescue if necessary. With a long line attached to the stern of the boat that was shooting the falls and the other end made fast to the one that was remaining above, a drag would be established, its weight depending on the muscle of the four men who would be rowing upstream.

When all was ready McBride and the professor took their places in the first boat. A few seconds after it had been pushed off the bar the current picked it up and swept it downriver. The four men at the end of the dragline put all they had into their oars. It checked the mad flight on the dancing shell that was now on the very brink of the plunge. There it seemed to stick, pounding up and down on the submerged rocks so violently that every second threatened to be its last.

A cry broke from the dry throats of the watchers on the bar as they saw McBride rise to his feet at risk of his neck and madly signal the men above to cast off the line. It was no sooner done than the released craft shot out over the crest and skittered across the swirling waters below.

"I guess we're next," Rainbow said.

"Yes," Itchi murmured. "Evidently a line is not feasible.
53

We shall have to shoot the falls." He turned to Grumpy. "Do you swim, Mr. Gibbs?"

"Like a muskrat!" the little one answered tartly.

With the speed of an express train they shot over the falls, striking a reef that splintered the oar in Grumpy's hands and left him clutching the useless handle. For a second they seemed to hang in space. A shudder ran over the boat as it struck the foaming water below.

Gass Labelle's ratty eyes met Itchi's. This was the moment for which they had waited. Timing it so that it appeared to have been an accident, they let their oars cross. In the second or two that the oars were hung up the boat veered off toward the dangerous ledges against which McBride had warned them. With Grumpy out of action it left only Rainbow with an oar in the water, and before he could check his stroke they were caught in a violent eddy that threw the boat on the fangs of a foam-lashed reef, ripping the side out as though it were made of paper.

Itchi and Labelle, thrown clear by the impact, looked back to see the boat turning turtle and dropping down on Rainbow and Grumpy. The latter realized their danger, too, and escaped being trapped by a miracle. Grumpy got away, but before Rainbow could strike out for shore a pair of yellow arms locked around his neck and he felt a knee being driven into his back. He tried to grab Itchi, throw him off, break that strangling hold before the Japanese drowned him, but he couldn't reach him.

Popeyed at what he saw, Grumpy raised the three-foot stub of the broken oar, and as the current swept him near he brought the club down on Itchi's head with a resounding thud.

"The danged yellow rat was tryin' to drown us!" the little man cried as the Japanese disappeared beneath the surface. "Labelle had his hand in it too! The whole thing was rigged!"

"Yeah," Rainbow gasped, filling his lungs with air. "I was about done for. Grab the Jap when he comes up and drag him ashore. I can make it by myself."

A few yards below the falls some pines, a dozen or more,

reared their lofty heads. There was level ground at their base and a short sandy beach. Grumpy dragged Itchi across it by the scruff of the neck and, with small liking for his task, went to work on him.

"He's coming around," Rainbow muttered. He could see Labelle scrambling over the rocks farther down the river. "Don't let on to either one of them, or to anyone else, that we know this wasn't an accident."

Itchi began to stir a few moments later. Ripley bent down and slapped the man's face sharply. It had the desired effect. "That did it! He'll be all right."

"By Christopher, it's a pity, if you ask me!" Grumpy observed sourly.

Itchi opened his eyes presently. "So sorry," he murmured. "I do not swim, Mr. Ripley. If my hold had not been broken both of us would have drowned. Fortunately your partner was near. I shall not forget this."

"Mr. Mouthful of Teeth, we ain't forgettin' it either!" Grumpy growled to himself.

Chapter Seven

THADDEUS HAMMERSLEY had witnessed the carefully planned accident to the partners' boat. Its unsatisfactory results left his face more hawklike than ever. The tension he was under—turning one face to Karen and the members of the expedition and meeting the threats to his secret plans with another—was beginning to tell on him. His piercing eyes burned with an insane intensity that had become more and more forbidding.

The other boats ran the falls with only minor damage. The professor waited until they were all down before he permitted himself to be rowed ashore.

"Ripley, when I saw you strike that ledge I thought everyone in your boat was done for. It shows what a little carelessness will lead to." His tone was sharp with annoyance. "I can't understand how you permitted yourselves to get caught like that. You had been warned explicitly."

Rainbow realized that this smooth attempt to put a virtuous face on the incident had a double purpose. Not only did it disclaim responsibility, but it was a subtle way of discovering whether Grumpy and he suspected the truth. He met it with guileless eyes.

"I don't know how it happened," he said. "My partner broke his oar. It seemed to throw the rest of us off timing. Before we could do anything we crashed."

"That is true, Doctor," Itchi spoke up. His tone was apologetic. "I'm afraid the fault was largely mine; I am not a skilled oarsman. The loss of the boat is a serious blow, I realize."

"Slick how the two of 'em work together," Grumpy told himself.

"We shall remain here and repair the boat," Hammersley stated. "We cannot afford to begin losing them at this stage of the descent."

The wrecked craft, kept afloat by its watertight compartments, had been pulled up on the beach. It was McBride's opinion that it could not be repaired. The professor refused to change his dictum, however, and ordered Brant to put his best men to work on the hull at once.

The prospect of spending several days here below the falls appealed to the various members of the expedition, providing the first real opportunity that Darwin and the others had had for exploration. The walls had fallen back so that any danger of sniping from above was eliminated. A careful examination of the strata in a side canyon, made with the aid of field glasses, proved so interesting to Borelius that he suggested that Darwin and Brant accompany him for the day. Jim fell in with the idea eagerly, and Brant, trapped by his talk of being a mining man, could only agree. Thursby was already moving down the shore line, a tripod and camera over his shoulder.

Suspecting Brant's predicament, Rainbow had to smile to himself as the three men began their long climb. He was still watching them when Grumpy came bustling up.

"We're goin' to row across the river," the little one announced. "Lots of quiet water a few yards down."

"We?" Ripley queried suspiciously.

"Miz Wattress——"

"Oh! Seems to me you're going in for art pretty strong." Rainbow showed him a frosty, reproving glance that didn't fool Grumpy for a second.

"Hunh!" the latter snorted. "That ain't the half of it! Reckon I got talents you never suspected. If there's anythin' you'd like to know about them old Eyetalian painters, I'll be able to tell you by the time we hit the saddle ag'in."

"I don't have to tell you our number is up," Ripley said in quite another tone. "We've forked our last bronc unless we keep our eyes open."

"You don't have to waste yore breath tellin' me," the little one growled. "I ain't feeble-minded! If they come at me ag'in, somebody's goin' to git a gun bent over his head!"

Rainbow walked down to the boat with Grumpy. They found Karen talking to Miss Wattress.

"Anne and I were just agreeing that we would not find anything more beautiful than this anywhere on the river," Karen told him. "It will be even more breath-taking when the afternoon shadows begin to play over the cliffs. Do you suppose I would be able to get a heavy camera up the wall three or four hundred feet?"

"I suppose you might find a place where it could be done," Rainbow said. "It would take time. If you want to have a try at it, I'll give you a hand."

"I'm afraid you've let yourself in for something," Anne Wattress laughed. "Karen has her eye on that deep bench halfway up to the rim."

Rainbow studied the wall for a minute or two. "Maybe we can reach it. If you'll agree to pack the lunch and a canteen, Karen," he said laughingly, "I'll promise to lug the camera."

The pleasantly warm day and the bright sunshine had a heartening effect on Karen. Ripley had never seen her so gay and carefree.

After being turned back several times Rainbow found a way up the wall. It was a hard, though not particularly dangerous, climb.

"This is glorious!" she cried as they reached the bench and she turned to drink in the view in every direction. "I'm going to squander plates recklessly!"

"Not until we've rested and had lunch," Rainbow advised. "We can stay here two hours. That will give us plenty of time to get down before dark."

Karen gave the occasion a holiday air. Rainbow found it contagious, and the tragedy and intrigue that were tightening their grip on the Hammersley Expedition were temporarily forgotten. The rich presence of this girl seemed to reach out and touch his world with a strange, pulsing ecstasy. In the end it brought him no peace, but he could easily understand why Jim Darwin was jealous of all men.

If Karen suspected the trend of Rainbow's thoughts she gave no sign of it. When she had exhausted the supply of dry plates she had brought along she saw him glance at his watch.

"I suppose it's time for us to be packing up," she said. Her tone was frankly regretful. "It's been a grand day. I've enjoyed every minute of it. I wish you were going all the way with us, Rainbow. I suppose when we say good-by in Brown's Park it will be the last we shall see of you."

"I hope not," he murmured. "You have a long way to go. I have a hunch I'll be running into you again." His intentions in this regard were more definite than he cared to put into words.

"I wish I could take that as a promise," Karen said frankly. "It would be nice to know that someone was looking out for us." He saw her square her shoulders resolutely as old misgivings assailed her.

"We'll make it a promise," Rainbow said with a sudden tightening of his lips. "If anything goes wrong I'll come after you and get you out."

Karen's eyes came up slowly and held his. Something ran between them as they stood there that was not to be put into words. The girl asked herself a question and could not answer it. But she had a deeper and clearer understanding of this tall man.

"Thank you," she whispered.

They returned to camp to find Darwin and the others back ahead of them. Supper was ready. As they ate, Hammersley was able to tell them that progress had been made in repairing the boat and that they would be able to leave late the following morning.

There was no reason why a fire could not be enjoyed. Later in the evening a full moon peered down into the canyon, adding a romantic touch. Darwin played on his mouth organ, and there was singing. Grumpy, who would have enjoyed the fun ordinarily, had too much on his mind to enter into it. Biding his time, he got Rainbow aside.

"Along with my art work, I picked up some facts today that'll come purty close to tellin' you what this business is all about," he began.

"Yeah?" Rainbow queried. "You sound serious enough. Since you got your information from Miss Wattress, I suppose your facts concern Karen."

"Yo're dead right!" the little fellow agreed sharply. "Did yuh know it was her money that's payin' for this grand splash?"

"No."

"Waal, it is! Hammersley's been operatin' on her bank account for a long time. Her father was one of these famous scientists too. Him and Hammersley dug up somethin' or other out in China years ago. Then he gits sick out there and dies, and when his will is read Hammersley is the executor and this Thane girl is his ward. She's just a little tot then, of course."

"Nothing so irregular about that," said Rainbow. "Where does the skulduggery come in that's got you all steamed up?"

"Jest wait!" Grumpy growled. "This Breckenridge Thane is a rich man; he leaves his daughter half a million or more. But the girl don't get her hands on none of it . . . not even when she grows up and comes of age. There's a clause in the will that makes Hammersley the administrator of the estate till she gets married. Waal, don't look at me as though you didn't know the answer! You jest got to put two and two together! Hammersley didn't have nuthin' till old Thane dies. Since then there's been Hammersley Expeditions all over the map!"

Ripley gave him a silencing glance. "Suppose we slow up a little and see what the facts add up to instead of going off half-cocked. Does Miss Wattress think Hammersley has been using the estate for his own ends?"

"Hell's fire, no! She thinks the old galoot is a hundred per cent all right. So does the girl! You can see how *she* trusts him. But we ain't swallowin' that with what we know." Grumpy lowered his voice at the sound of footsteps. Two of Brant's men strolled down the shore. He waited until they were out of earshot. "Now I'll tell you somethin' else. Hammersley's done his best to keep that girl from marryin'. He's been luggin' her off with him for three or four years. But this young Darwin wouldn't have it that way. Miz Wattress says they're engaged . . . or close to it."

"So I figured." In the shadows Rainbow's mouth had a grim set.

"That all you got to say?" Grumpy demanded fiercely. "Do you mean to tell me you can't see that it's the girl them wolves is after? Hammersley don't intend to lose his easy pickin's. That girl will never leave these canyons alive!"

"No," Rainbow disagreed. "That wouldn't explain all these elaborate preparations."

"Wouldn't it? If we had been rubbed out this mornin'

who could have said it wasn't jest an accident? There'll be more accidents, I'm tellin' you! Murder without a kickback, jest because the perfessor was smart enough to dress it up with all these trimmin's!"

Ripley shook his head. "I can't believe it . . . not that I'd put it past Hammersley and the Jap. But that isn't the full extent of their game. It couldn't be. There's Brant and Morgan. They're all out for something too. It couldn't be Karen."

"I don't know why it couldn't," the hardheaded little man persisted. "Brant and the perfessor is stickin' together till they get rid of us. Labelle proved that to us this mornin'. But Brant's goin' to take charge of things when the time's right. He'll grab the girl and hold her till he gets his price . . . unless Blue beats him to it."

Rainbow was ready to dismiss the whole thing as utterly fantastic. "You'll find that Blue has something else on his mind, and the others too," he said flatly.

"Mebbe," Grumpy snapped. "It's a danged good idea to remember that some gents have more'n one string to their bow, an' I'm thinkin' of Hammersley an' the Jap when I say it." He gritted his teeth savagely. "If I'm only a third right it's righter than I want to be about this."

By ten o'clock the next morning the expedition was under way. The declivity became greater, and although the boats passed through one series of rapids after another the rapids were not of a nature to give them any trouble. The boats seemed to fly along. Without stopping they ran past a beautiful little valley. Grumpy identified it as Little Brown's Hole.

The canyon walls continued to rise to a great height, but in an ever-widening V, until it was possible to glimpse their battlemented rims. On those rocky turrets wind and frost had been busy for centuries. Untold tons of decaying granite seemed to totter there, waiting for a breath to send them plunging into the canyon.

The thought occurred to Rainbow as the No. 2 boat drifted slowly down the river with only Labelle's heavy steering oar in the water. Itchi glanced aloft too. "It is an awe-inspiring sight, Mr. Ripley," the Japanese murmured. "If those frowning ramparts were to come tumbling down they would crash an ocean leviathan."

"Yeah," Rainbow muttered. There had been little conversation in the boat that day.

"Rapide!" Labelle called a warning as white water appeared ahead.

Ripley was running his oar through the rowlock when a shrill cry broke from Itchi's lips. It was the first time the partners had heard him raise his voice. The next instant a muffled thunder rolled down to them. Their eyes flashed to the rim where a puff of white smoke hung in the air. The next instant a whole section of the crumbling, fancifully carved rimrock teetered drunkenly, as though trying to catch its balance, and then plunged forward and downward, into space.

"Dynamite!" Grumpy yelled in Rainbow's ear.

Their own boat was out of danger. A warning cry to the others was wasted, but they were alive to their position and could do nothing to save themselves. Ripley's eyes froze as he saw Karen's boat nearest of all to the base of the wall. A shudder seemed to run over the river as the mighty avalanche of rock struck the lower slope of the cliff, a hundred feet above the water line. Rainbow saw great boulders, weighing tons, pop up into the air from that impact and sail out over the river in a wide, terrifying arc.

In near the wall a rain of small rocks fell.

"They're all right in there!" Grumpy yelled. "But look at Potts and Thursby!"

The No. 7 boat had been caught directly in the path of destruction. A tremendous shaft of rock struck the river within a foot or two of the bow, sending up a great spout of water that stood the frail shell on end. Two of Brant's men, Poe and Fancher, were in the boat with Thursby and Dr. Potts. Thursby and Poe managed to hang on; Potts and the other man sailed through the air as though they had been catapulted from a springboard.

The boat fell back, and its wide beam saved it from capsizing, but as it settled down on the writhing river another boulder of equal size caught it full amidships, crushing it like an eggshell and carrying it to the bottom.

"Come on!" Rainbow shouted. "We've got to get back there and pick them up!"

McBride already had his boat turned, and though rocks of smaller size, but carrying death to whatever they struck, continued to fall for several minutes, he ordered his crew to strike back up the river. They picked up Chick Fancher a few moments before Rainbow reached Dr. Potts. He brought the little man in looking like a dripping, badly frightened water spaniel. There was no sign of Thursby and Poe or the smashed boat.

"They're at the bottom of the river!" Grumpy ground out. "Luckily Darwin has sense enough to keep them boats with the wimin in where they are!"

"I'm going to send them down the river," Rainbow said with authority as Hammersley came alongside. "We're only two or three miles from Brown's Park. They'll be out of danger there."

The professor, cheeks sunken and white of face, nodded his agreement. "This has been a terrible experience, Ripley," he said, striving to regain his composure. "That wall must have been rotten to the core to topple down on us like that." `

Rainbow's eyes ran cold with fury at the brazen attempt to give the tragedy the appearance of having been a natural accident. "Nothing of the sort," he said thinly. "It's time for some plain speaking between us, Professor. That wall was blasted out. You know why Morgan is determined to stop you. I don't expect you to tell me, but it's plain enough that that's what he is out to do. That's why he tried to steal your boats at Black Forks. That's why Brant was almost picked off at the falls. If you want to risk your life on this river that's

63

your business, but the members of the expedition have got to be told where they stand."

"Mr. Ripley, has it occurred to you that the presence of you and Mr. Gibbs may explain Blue Morgan's murderous attempts on us?" Itchi was quick to ask.

"It has," Rainbow answered. "That may be the answer." Grumpy was hard put to swallow his surprise. A moment later, however, he thought he understood his partner's purpose. "When you get to Brown's Park stay there," he heard Rainbow say. "Give us four or five days. We'll take care of Morgan!"

Chapter Eight

COME ON, Labelle," Rainbow ordered. "We're pulling into the wall!"

Big Gass hesitated, and his eyes went to Samson Brant. It was a clear-cut indication of where the Frenchman felt authority rested. Brant's glance told him to do as he had been directed. He followed it with a question to Rainbow. "How far down the park are you going?"

"The sooner we reach the Gate the better," Ripley informed him. "If we're going to make it before evening tomorrow we'll have to run down to the mouth of Beaver Creek today."

"We'll be looking for you there," Brant said gruffly. "Don't make yourselves too hard to find." It carried a threat and a warning.

The contemptuous look that flirted across Itchi's yellow face eloquently expressed his low regard for such cheap blustering.

"You all right in here?" Rainbow called out as they came up to the three boats that had found shelter near the wall, his glance going to Karen first of all.

"Yes," Darwin answered him. "I seem to be the only one

64

who got a scratch." There was a smear of blood on his chin. "But look at that!" He pointed to a hole in the forward bulkhead a few inches from Karen. A man could have put his head into it, and it was as sharply cut as though the work had been done with a saw.

The compartment was filled with water, the rock having passed completely through the bottom of the boat. Rainbow's eyes narrowed grimly as he surveyed the damage and realized how close Karen had been to being killed.

"We're going to get out of here," he said, rasing his voice so all might hear. "Keep in close to the wall for a mile or two. We're just above Brown's Park. We'll come out into a valley five to six miles wide. Just follow us!" He turned to Jim. "You used your head that time. How did you manage to get in so quickly?"

"I saw the puff of smoke go up a second or two before I heard the explosion. I guess it's all that saved us."

"Rainbow, isn't there any chance that Lee Thursby and the other man may be found alive?" Karen asked. Her voice had a tense, unfamiliar tone.

Ripley shook his head. "McBride thinks they may be able to recover the bodies by waiting. They're going to stay here awhile."

Dreading a repetition of the disaster, Rainbow kept the boats in so close to shore that it was often possible to reach it with the oars. He didn't try to hide the sigh. of relief that escaped his tight lips when they ran out of Red Canyon into the valley of Brown's Park. The river lost its mad rush and the current became so sluggish that it was necessary to use the oars continuously.

"We'll go ashore at the first likely spot," Ripley told Labelle. "That boat of Darwin's is settling pretty low in the water. We can make some temporary repairs."

The cook and his pots and pans had been left up the river in one of the boats that had remained at the scene of the accident, but emergency rations were available.

"The men are hungry; I suppose we should prepare something," Karen said to Rainbow. "Anne and I will attend to it."

Grumpy volunteered his assistance, and he soon had a small fire burning. "This ain't the first time Rainbow and me have stuck our nose into this ole outlaw hangout," he told Karen and Anne Wattress. "It's a right purty spot, summer or winter!"

The glades opening between the trees, carpeted with grass, had a parklike look and readily suggested how the valley had come by its name.

"It's a paradise," Anne declared. "It seems hard to believe it was once a rendezvous for rustlers and horse thieves. It looks innocent enough now."

"I don't know about that, Miz Anne," Rainbow overheard Grumpy answer. "Brown's Park has seen all kinds, but I reckon the worst of 'em couldn't hold a candle to some of the murderin', double-crossin' hombres that's usin' this country today."

Ripley knew his partner was referring to Hammersley and his fellow conspirators. He saw a question form in Anne Wattress' eyes that made him wonder if she, too, wasn't close to understanding Grumpy's thinly veiled remark.

Repairs to the boat and lunch consumed an hour. The others not having put in an appearance as yet, Rainbow gave the word to proceed down the river.

"You don't figger they've run into more trouble, do you?" Grumpy queried as he paused from laboring with the oars to mop his perspiring face. The afternoon had turned unseasonably warm.

Itchi did not turn his head, but he hung on Ripley's answer.

"If you mean another rock slide, no," the latter said. "We would have been sure to hear it. They'll have to bury Thursby and Poe. That'll take some time."

This open country, the almost placid river, and the release from immediate danger revived the spirits of all. They reached the mouth of the Beaver and made camp, however, without

seeing anything of the professor and the others who had remained with him. Ripley saw that Karen was troubled.

"You're sure they're all right?" she asked.

"Yes," Rainbow told her. "It may be midnight before they
show up. We'll keep a fire going for them."

Though he dismissed it so lightly to her, he had begun
to wonder if Brant had taken advantage of this division of
forces to take things into his own hands. Rainbow suspected
that something of the sort was running through Saburo Itchi's
facile brain. But there were four of Brant's men here in camp.
They were stretched out on the grass, smoking their pipes and
casting interested glances at the fire where supper was being
cooked. After watching them for a few minutes he was satisfied that they didn't have the look of men waiting to spring
a surprise.

Itchi was silent through the meager supper. "I am going to
climb that dead tree at the water's edge, Mr. Ripley," he
announced as he got up. "I should be able to see some distance up the river; it's still light enough."

"Go ahead," Rainbow told him. "You may be able to see
them coming."

Grumpy stepped aside with his partner. "The Jap is worried," he muttered.

"So am I, but not about Hammersley and Brant getting
here," Rainbow informed him. "Howie Hallett should be
waiting with our horses down by the Gate tomorrow. That
will bring things to a head with us. We're going to have
trouble getting away. We know too much. If we're permitted
to leave, it will only be because we've sold them the idea that
we can keep Blue out of their way. That would help their
game. They'll weigh it against whatever trouble they feel we
might make them."

"Yeah," the little one grunted. "That's about the size of
our chances. Brant won't fall for it, though. He showed where
he stood this mornin' when you made that crack about goin'
after Blue."

"I know it," Rainbow muttered, his lean face sober and tight of lip. "Itchi is our best bet. We'll make our play now . . . as soon as he climbs out of that tree."

A shout from the Japanese announced that he could see the boats coming. In the deepening twilight he came back to the log where Rainbow and Grumpy sat. The partners pretended to have their heads together and not to be aware of his approach. Ripley had the small square of goods he had cut from Chink Johnson's shirt in his hands. He made it appear that he was examining it carefully, and, as Itchi stepped up, he hurriedly tried to conceal it, only to let the piece slip through his fingers.

He bent down to retrieve it, but the Japanese reached it first.

"Is this what you are looking for, Mr. Ripley?" Itchi questioned suspiciously.

"Yeah!" Rainbow reached out for it, but the Oriental had recognized the bright-colored sample.

"I think I know where this came from, Mr. Ripley," he murmured. His tone suggested that the discovery amused him, but his eyes told another story. "I saw that someone had cut a piece out of Johnson's shirt. I wondered who had found it so interesting."

"Interesting is putting it mildly," Rainbow said with chilling inflection. "That piece of wool will send Blue Morgan to the pen!"

Itchi gazed at him with his blank eyes for a moment, his face expressionless. "Would you explain, please?"

Ripley handed him the sample he had received from the Wasatch Mills. "You see that they match. A shipment of those shirts was on the freight train that was wrecked at Split Mountain. It is a pattern that has not yet been placed on sale out here. Yet Johnson was wearing one."

The Japanese nodded woodenly. "He therefore must have been responsible for the wrecking of the train. Perhaps one of a gang. Obviously he helped himself to a new shirt." He handed the samples over to Rainbow. "Your story of the wreck being the result of a grudge was incorrect, I see."

"It was an attempt to stop one of the silk expresses . . . a carefully planned attempt that misfired only because the express had been laid up with a minor accident and the freight was running on her time. Blue Morgan doesn't stick up freight trains."

It was a broadside shot, but Itchi's only sign of surprise was a more pronounced display of his heavy white teeth.

"Does that satisfy your curiosity?" Rainbow demanded thinly. He was still playing his part.

"Completely."

"O.K.! But don't ever slip up in back of me again without letting me know you're there. I don't like it." To put a sharper edge on his annoyance, Rainbow turned his back on the Japanese and walked over to the fire.

In a few minutes the boats could be seen approaching. On arriving, Hammersley quickly confirmed Rainbow's surmise as to what had held them up. They had found Thursby and Poe and buried them in Red Canyon.

The camp was quiet that night. Everyone seemed glad to reach his blankets. Grumpy had bedded down beside Rainbow.

"You almost knocked the legs out from under Itchi," the little man muttered beneath his breath. "You couldn't have handled it better. Him and Hammersley and Brant was certainly talkin' things up tonight. If it was us they was palaverin' about they shore couldn't agree on nuthin'."

"All we can do is be ready for tomorrow, no matter what it brings," Ripley said, yawning.

Running down through Brown's Park the next day proved uneventful. In the early afternoon they caught their first glimpse of the unrivaled Gate of Lodore. That magnificent portal, dark and lonely in its flawless grandeur, cut back into the very heart of the mountains and seemed to hold the secrets of a world beyond.

The great cleft, visible for many miles, made Karen, now the expedition's only photographer, and Anne Wattress, with her artist's eye, forget the hardships and dangers of the descent. Camera and sketchbook were in evidence all afternoon.

It had ben agreed that camp would be made at Vermilion Creek. As the boats swung around the almost complete circle the river describes just above the mouth of the Vermilion, a man on horseback hailed them from the bank.

"It's Howie Hallett, all right!" Grumpy exclaimed in quick identification. He sent an answering cry to the Bar 7 rider.

A few minutes later McBride ordered the boats to run ashore, where camp could be made in a grove of tall cottonwoods.

"I've got the horses back on the grass a few hundred yards," Hallett told the partners. "If you're goin' to camp here I'll bring 'em up."

"Leave 'em where they are, Howie," Rainbow advised. The gravity of his tone made the puncher raise a sharply questioning pair of eyes.

"What's the matter, Rip? You and Grump wear out your welcome with these people?"

"I'll explain that to you later," Rainbow told him. "You stick around, Howie, and keep your eyes open. We'll leave here tonight, and we may be traveling fast when we do. I'll see Hammersley now."

The professor was with Brant and Itchi, Rainbow rightly suspected that he and Grumpy were the subject of their acrimonious discussion.

"We'll be pulling away after supper," Ripley told them. "We can reach the railroad by morning and get the horses and ourselves carried across the river to Vernal. I know where to start looking for Morgan."

"Where?" Brant watched him with scowling eyes.

"Ute Crossing. He's got a saloon there. It's a hangout for his gang."

"And you think you'll find them waiting there for you, eh?" Brant made no attempt to hide his contempt.

"They may have drifted," Rainbow acknowledged. "But we've picked up a few trails in our time. We'll either grab

70

Morgan or keep him so busy he won't have any time to devote to the Hammersley Expedition."

His tone didn't admit of there being any question about his leaving. Brant had no more to say, but the professor thanked Rainbow for his services and spoke regretfully of their having to part company.

Ripley left them, and he was no sooner out of hearing than Itchi declared himself. "Mr. Ripley is very clever," he said, "but he does not fool me. He evidently hopes to arrest Morgan, then turn his attention to us."

"Sure!" Brant agreed. It was the first time he had ever aligned himself with the Japanese. "If we stay here four or five days as he suggests, it would only be giving him time to square off at us. Why couldn't he and Gibbs have been in that No. 7 boat instead of Thursby and Poe? Until that pair is put out of the way we can't draw a safe breath!"

"But there would be a twofold advantage in having them busily chasing Morgan's gang," Itchi continued, quite as though Brant had not spoken. "It would remove two obstacles from our path at one stroke, Doctor. That might outweigh the risk involved in permitting Ripley and Gibbs to leave."

"It would be the grossest stupidity to think otherwise," Hammersley pronounced, his piercing eyes taking fire. "It would give us a free hand for a few days. It is not necessary for us to remain here. We can start through Lodore in the morning."

"You're crazy . . . both of you!" Brant burst out wrathfully. "I've got my neck in this as deep as either one of you, and I'm going to have something to say about what goes on here. If Ripley and Gibbs make any attempt to leave I'll stop them!"

The professor turned his baleful eyes on him. "You forget yourself, Mr. Brant," he said with chilling inflection. "I do not believe I underestimate the danger involved in permitting the two men to depart. When this month's Silk Express is stopped they will suspect us. But that is something we must risk. We shall work swiftly, and we shall leave no clue for

71

them to follow. Six to eight hours after we get the silk in our possession we'll have it hidden away where no one will find it. If it has to stay there a year before we can begin to realize on it we'll be patient and wait. The mistake above all others that we can not afford to make is one I had not dreamed of until a few days ago."

"Yes, I think I know what you mean, Doctor," Itchi murmured unctuously. "Having accomplished all the necessary steps, it would be very embarrassing to discover at the last moment that someone else—shall we say Blue Morgan?—had got in ahead of us and stopped the Silk Express."

It was answer enough for Brant. Snarling to himself, he made his way across the camp to his men.

Hammersley and Itchi exchanged a long, understanding glance.

"The man will have to be put in his place," the professor said bluntly.

Itchi nodded. "I shall attend to it, Doctor."

This camp in Brown's Park was the pleasantest they had made so far, but no one seemed to be in a mood to enjoy it. When supper was over Karen walked to the boats. Rainbow followed in the dusk of the deepening twilight.

"You know I hate to see you go," she said with a complete frankness.

"It will be nice to be missed," he murmured, his thoughts running ahead of his words. The tone of his voice brought Karen's eyes up, bright and touched with wondering. For a moment they stood there engrossed, saying nothing.

"I didn't mean it quite that way, Rainbow. I . . . I've come to depend on you. There's strength in you. I'm sure I'm not the only one of us who has felt it. Things are not right here. Uncle and Mr. Brant are close to breaking."

"Nothing will come of it," he said with quiet conviction. "The professor is the strong man of the two. And don't underestimate Itchi. There'll be some more switching of crews when you leave here. Don't let them take Jim or Dr. Borelius out of your boat. Promise me that," he insisted, enormously

72

sober of a sudden. "Do what they tell you. You can depend on both of them. I'll make it my business to be in Island Park before you get there. If you don't show up after a day or two I'll start looking for you."

"You have my promise," she said quietly, offering him her hand. Rainbow took it and stood there, a tall, square shape in the twilight. He envied Jim Darwin this girl, and it put a sadness in him that he didn't want her to see.

"I'm going to stay here a minute, Rainbow," Karen said. "Good-by."

Halfway back to camp, Ripley came face to face with Darwin. The coolness of the other's greeting needed no explanation.

"Don't get me wrong, Jim," Ripley told him. "I'm not trying to beat your time. I just told Karen not to let either you or Borelius be taken out of her boat and to look to you if something goes wrong. Do you have a gun?"

"Yes."

"Well, wear it from now on."

Darwin let him go, only to call him back. "Rainbow, I'm still acting like an ass. I'm sorry. Have you got anything else to tell me?"

Ripley gave him a long, measuring glance. "You can take this any way you please. Don't put your trust in Hammersley or the Jap."

Leaving Jim standing there, Rainbow joined Grumpy. A few minutes later they reached Howie Hallett and the waiting horses.

"You must've had things sized up wrong. Everythin's calm and peaceful," Howie said.

He spoke too soon. Suddenly Brant and seven of his men stepped out of the brush and closed in on them on the run. It was too late to reach the saddles and try to break away. Even as Rainbow dismissed that thought fists began to fly. Fancher and Revell tried to drag Grumpy down, but they found they had got hold of a fighting wildcat. The little man doubled Fancher up with a kick in the belly and turned in time to drive a smashing fist into Ginger Revell's long chin.

Rainbow realized this was not a fight; Brant's orders were to pull them down and tie them up. Brant tried to smother him, but a long whistling right drove him back. Howie was more than holding his own too. But the odds were too one-sided to leave the result long in doubt.

The next moment help came from an unexpected source. Rainbow saw a man dart out from between the nervous horses and catch Revell by the shoulders and toss him over his head. It drove Brant and the others back. Saburo Itchi stood there, a gun in his leveled hand.

"My marksmanship hardly can be compared with yours, Mr. Brant," he said, his tone inflexible and apologetic at the same time, "but I could hardly miss at this distance. These men will be permitted to leave. That is Dr. Hammersley's order."

Chapter Nine

ONCE THE partners and Hallett had climbed out of Brown's Park Rainbow struck off across a broken mountain plateau that brought them back to within several miles of the river. There they rolled into their blankets for a few hours. Silverbow, a flag stop ten miles east of the Green, was their ultimate destination, but when dawn broke they swung even farther to the west and reached the rim high above the Canyon of Lodore. This maneuver had but one purpose, and the morning was still young when it rewarded them with a definite answer. Far up the canyon they could see the boats coming.

"Wait three or four days?" Grumpy burst out sarcastically. "Why, we didn't no more'n have our backs turned before they was sneakin' down the river! If we didn't know no more'n this it would tell us enough! It ain't only Blue Morgan that they're tryin' to run away from!"

Rainbow agreed fully. "It doesn't leave us much time," he said gravely.

They could see Upper Disaster Falls in the distance, a long series of rapids terminating in a sharp drop. From the head of the white water to the dangerous sag below the falls the descent was fully fifty feet. With a twenty-mile current driving it, the river seemed to be torn to milky shreds. Seen from the rim, this beginning of Hell's Half Mile was a scene of wild, incomparable beauty, its thunder rising in a deafening roar.

"We'll wait a minute!" Rainbow shouted. "I want to see what McBride's going to do about this!"

Down in the half-mile-deep trough of Lodore the boats seemed to be just so many plunging match sticks. Rainbow and Grumpy saw McBride frantically drive the lead boat into the west bank. When it appeared that they could not make it the crew leaped into the water, found footing and dragged the boat ashore, then turned to catch the others as they swept in.

"Unloadin'!" Grumpy called out. "Goin' to work the boats down along the shore empty!"

Rainbow nodded, visibly relieved. "They'll run Lodore all right if they use their heads that way! Well, I guess we can be pulling out for the railroad!"

A station and some seldom-used shipping pens were the extent of Silverbow. Noon had come and gone before the partners caught their first glimpse of it.

"You goin' to try an' git in touch with Moran?" Grumpy queried. "I reckon he's wonderin' what we're doin'."

"I'll send him a wire," answered Rainbow. "If we went into Platte City it would take time, and Tom might not approve of slapping Yampa Jackson into jail just to throw Morgan off the scent. Corporations don't like damage suits."

"A damage suit from that old owl hoot?" Grumpy scoffed.

75

"Why, that grease-caked buzzard has busted every law in the book!"

The agent dispatched Ripley's telegram and agreed to flag the first local freight that would carry them across the river into Utah.

"I guess this is where I say so long," Howie told the partners. "This came just at the right time," he grinned. "I missed the worst of the spring work; the roundup wagon was just startin' out when I left the ranch. Time I get back——"

"Howie, you'll do just as well by going across the river with us and finding your way home over Ute Pass," Rainbow cut in. "Suppose you stick around a few days. You may come in handy. I'll square it with the judge."

Howie rubbed his long, humorous nose. "Well, I don't mind lookin' at a little trouble if I got the right tools for it in my hand. I'll string along, Rip."

"You're a stranger around Vernal?" Ripley asked.

"Yeah."

"Fine! We'll have you put off out in the hills somewhere. You drift into town then and don't give anyone any reason to think we're friends. I fancy we'll be watched soon after we arrive. If we want to get in touch with you, or you with us, we'll have to be careful how we go about it."

Three days later the partners located Yampa Jackson near the Uinta Agency. They immediately swore out a warrant against him and assisted the sheriff in serving it. Vehemently protesting his innocence, the old man was slapped into jail, accused of responsibility for the Split Mountain wreck.

The news reached Blue Morgan at Ute Crossing a few hours later. Yampa's arrest didn't interest the outlaw as much as the fact that Rainbow and Grumpy had left the Hammersley Expedition and were back in Utah.

"They must've split up in Brown's Park," Morgan told Ben Ruby, who had brought him the news. "It's the only place where they could've got out."

"Blue, where does that leave us?" Ben asked. He had lived outside the law most of his life and had grown tough and

76

shrewd in the process. "Slappin' old Yampa into the cala-
boose don't sound on the level to me. Ripley an' Gibbs are
workin' for the railroad, ain't they? If they'd gone after the
old coot when they was here two weeks ago it would have
been different. I could have believed that. I'd have said they
was just makin' a dumb play. After all, they ain't no smarter
than anybody else. But instead they go prancin' off with them
boats."

"I don't know, Ben," Morgan declared weightily as he
paced up and down behind his bar. "If that pair is dumb
enough to let Brant pull the wool over their eyes they may
figger Yampa is the party they've been after." His upper lip
curled away from his teeth in a characteristic gesture. "Whatever it is, it's no skin off our noses! They're not comin' back
with anythin' on us. Sure they know Chink was lined up with
me. He got killed tryin' to steal their boats. But maybe he
was on his own. Why should I know anythin' about it?"

Ruby pushed back his hat and scratched his bald head,
doubt riding him. "They know somebody came mighty near
knockin' Brant off," he muttered skeptically. "They know half
a mountain was dumped on 'em. You mean to tell me they'll
miss suspectin' us?"

"Let 'em," Blue sneered. "They can't prove nothin'." He
ran a cold eye over Ben Ruby, Wild Bill, and the others lined
up along the bar and realized that they were not convinced.
"You boys are forgettin' that Ripley and his pardner ain't
got no reason to think I know Brant from Adam."

"Yo're right," Wild Bill Williams declared. "That's somethin' we overlooked. But this thing shouldn't be allowed to
drift along, Blue——"

"I don't aim to let it," Morgan whipped out. "I'll ride
into Vernal tomorrow and be lookin' for a face down. You
got someone keepin' an eye on 'em?"

"Yeah, Crutcher and three or four others," Ben told him.

"Suppose the rest of you drift in now," Blue advised.
"We'll have backin' enough to see it through however it goes.
What Ripley doesn't say will give us a line on what's up.

77

If he doesn't make a crack about Chink and what happened in Red Canyon, you can be doggoned sure that juggin' Yampa is just a gag to throw dust in our eyes."

Morgan arrived in Vernal about noon of the following day. He rode with a confident swagger, and men on the street turned to watch him with a remote, furtive interest.

From the hotel window Grumpy and Rainbow saw him rack his horse in front of the saloon opposite and disappear between the swinging doors. They knew they were being watched and had been for twenty-four hours. They were also aware of the presence of Ben Ruby, Tay Crutcher, Wild Bill, and all the rest of Blue's cohorts.

"He's here to ask 'How come?'" Grumpy observed, his hard-bitten face settling into deeper lines. "'Pears to me we've got all our eggs in one basket this time, and she's a basket with a weak handle."

"What do you mean?" Rainbow asked without shifting his gaze from the saloon. Howie Hallett leaned his lanky length against one of the uprights that supported the wooden awning in front of the place. Rainbow nodded to Howie, and the latter immediately followed Blue inside. Grumpy got all this.

"I mean we can't play too innocent or that bunch will smell a mouse," he muttered. "We're supposed to be sittin' back now, waitin' for Morgan to make a move that'll lead us to Hammersley and Brant and crack things wide open in general. He'll never do it if we act fishy."

"We'll walk in over there with a proper chip on our shoulder," the other answered. "Come on!"

Rainbow led the way across the tawny dust of Vernal's main street with a long stride. Behind the saloon's swinging doors the head and shoulders of Ben Ruby disappeared at once.

"Blue doesn't intend to be surprised," was Ripley's thought. Stepping through the doors, he let his glance run to the corners of the barroom and back, and its details were stamped on his brain with photographic clearness. Blue stood with his back to the bar, elbows on the rail. Ruby and the others were

78

conveniently arranged on either side of him. Howie sat in a chair, his hat on his lap, looking as though he had no concern with what went on about him. There had been noise, empty laughter here a moment before. It was gone now, and Rainbow saw unmistakable signs of tension in the dark faces turned toward him. The pattern of this moment was a thoroughly familiar one. A faint hint of a smile touched his tightly clamped lips as he pondered the fact that Morgan found reinforcements of such size necessary.

"I'm glad you rode in, Blue," he said with sharp hostility. "It'll save me the bother of looking you up."

"Is that so?" Morgan inquired, lips barely moving. "I didn't know there was anythin' you had to see me about."

"Then maybe I can refresh your memory. I don't know what you've got against the Hammersley Expedition, and I don't care. Maybe it's what they think . . . that you're just trying to square what happened to Chink Johnson. That was my idea when you started sniping at Brant."

"Forget it, Ripley," Blue jeered. "I don't know nothin' about this Hammersley bunch except what I read in the newspaper."

Rainbow ignored the interruption. "You've been on the wrong side of the fence ever since I've known you, Blue, but I always figured you were a cut above the ordinary run of blacklegs I've had to deal with. I changed my mind about that when you sent that wall tumbling down on us. There were women in those boats; they might have been drowned as well as the two men who got it.

"Fairy tales!" Morgan pretended to be amused. "If you had anythin' like that on me you wouldn't be around here talkin' about it. You'd have a warrant out, and you'd be busy gettin' it served."

"You're right," Rainbow acknowledged. "We know the evidence we have against you won't stand up in court. Suppose we forget the law and make this personal."

He felt rather than saw Morgan's men draw apart and loosen up. Grumpy stepped back too. Ripley read the movement for what it was—the usual prelude to a quick draw. Across the barroom Howie Hallett leaned back in his chair, his hat still in his lap, and pretended to have only a bored, obscure interest in the argument. Blue read these things with equal understanding.

"Sure," he muttered, his slitted, opaque eyes enormously alert. He knew Howie had a gun in his lap under his hat. It left the odds all on Blue's side, but he didn't want a gunplay out of this, and he was ready to do a little crawling to avoid it. He had come to town to get some information. It was his now, and he didn't intend to waste it here. "That's pretty clever of you, Ripley." Blue's laugh was a grating effort. "You'd like to catch me with a gun, wouldn't you, knowin' I'm on parole? But this will keep for another time. Tell your friend over there in the chair to put on his hat and slip his gun back into the holster. It might go off and hurt him." He jerked his head at Ben Ruby and the others. "Come on, boys! We got some business down the street."

They started out, but Rainbow stepped in Morgan's way. "Blue, the yellow streak in you gets wider by the minute."

It was almost too much for Morgan. His lips twitched murderously, and for a moment the issue again hung in doubt. But in some far-off corner of Blue's brain a warning bell rang. "That's a mouthful you'll have to eat some day, Ripley," he growled, "and you'll get the bellyache doin' it!"

Rainbow let him go. From the doorway he saw the man turn into a saloon farther down the street.

"I don't git it," declared Grumpy, shaking a puzzled head. "That's not Blue's speed to let you put the crawl on him like that. He must have somethin' mighty important on his mind that he ain't goin' to be shaken loose from."

"No question about it," Rainbow agreed. "But I'm satisfied. He figures he got about all we know. That's what he was after. I predict that crowd won't be around town long now."

"But how did he spot me?" Howie demanded unhappily. "I thought I had that bunch euchred."

"One of his spies," Rainbow answered. "The town seems

80

to be full of 'em. Every move we make is going to be watched. It means that when that bunch slips away and we go tagging after them they'll be sure to know it."

"Why can't we cross 'em up by leavin' here the same way we come?" Grumpy demanded. "No trick to have the hosses put in a boxcar and have the railroad dump us out in the brush where we want to get off. That bunch won't do nuthin' till they've had a big powwow, and that'll take 'em back to Ute Crossin' for a day or two."

"It'll be taking a chance on losing them altogether," Ripley answered. "But anything will be better than being cooped up here with our hands tied, and that way we can get Howie out of this too."

"No, Rip!" Hallett protested. "I'm seein' this through! Morgan hurt my feelin's when he showed me up. I ain't so simple as all that."

"All right," Rainbow agreed. "They know you now, Howie. They'll stop you just as quick as they would Grumpy or me. The two of you go down to the station and tell the agent what you want. I'll settle up at the hotel. Don't bother with trying to hide what we're doing. Morgan will know before we even get the horses loaded."

The dispatch with which the news reached Blue fully justified Ripley's observation. The outlaw professed to find it to his liking.

"Boys, they're doin' just what I told you they would," he declared confidently. "They don't intend to lose sight of us. Ten, twelve hours from now they'll be watchin' Ute Crossin'. And that's exactly what I want 'em to be doin'! Just so they'll be sure they'll find us there, we'll head back right now!"

Morgan had not lost face with his crowd over the incident in the saloon. In fact, the reverse was true. Thanks to the way he had handled the situation, they believed they knew where they stood now. Blue summed it up for them as they rode north.

"We can forget about that freight wreck. Mad as Ripley was, he'd have made some crack about it if he and Gibbs suspected us. They'll prosecute old Yampa, and that'll be the end of it." He laughed disparagingly. "That pair would ride you into the ground if you was doin' a little rustlin'. But that's about the size of 'em. They're way over their heads on anythin' like this. Why, they were in those boats for ten days with Brant and never tumbled to what's up!"

Ben Ruby wagged his bald head. "Leastwise they got savvy enough in 'em to know who was givin' them boats hell."

"And smart enough to know there ain't anythin' they can do about it," Blue snapped.

He had no more to say, and whenever a question was put to him his answer was to shut up, that he was thinking. That evening in Ute Crossing he startled his men by announcing that he was changing his plans.

"Yeah, I mean it," he told them. "Instead of tryin' to smash Brant we're goin' to help him. We know what the boats are for. We'll give that bunch a chance to use 'em."

"Blue, yo're crazy!" Wild Bill Williams objected furiously. "If the Silk Express is stopped this month we'll never get another crack at her! Yuh was right when yuh said our play was to let things quiet down for a time . . . stop Brant or anyone else who tried to start somethin'!"

"Sure I was right," Morgan agreed. "But I got somethin' better now. What's wrong with lettin' them fellers make the haul and cache the stuff. They'll have to hide it out in a hurry. Where could they find a better place than Island Park? The silk'll be hot; they'll have to leave it there a few weeks. That'll give us all the time we want. We'll just take the stuff away from them. Ain't that easier than grabbin' it off the railroad company?"

"Blue, yo're a whiz!" Ben Ruby declared admiringly. The others were equally impressed. Only Wild Bill remained unconvinced.

"What about Ripley and Gibbs? Mebbe they don't figger there's anythin' queer about that expedition, but they shore expect us to have another try at bustin' it up, and they'll be out to stop us."

"Of course they will! That's what they'll be hangin' around for." Blue glared him to silence. "I got that figured out, if you'll let me finish. We've got to be sure that bunch over on the river has a free hand. A week will be time enough; the express will be through before then. That means we've got to keep Ripley and his friends busy, don't it?"

"Yeah——"

"Well, if we did a sneak out of here don't you figure they'd follow us?"

Wild Bill began to see it. A slow, crafty smile spread over his leathery face. "That's slick, Blue! Mighty slick! They'll go for it like a trout after a fly!"

"You bet they will!" Morgan grinned. "We'll go down through the Painted Bluffs and strike toward the river once or twice; that'll needle 'em up. Once we get below the railroad, we'll pull 'em all the way down across the San Blas Plateau. As long as we can make them believe we're tryin' to shake them off they'll keep comin' after us. By the time they take a tumble to themselves the silk train will have been knocked off, and they'll be our ironclad alibi that we didn't have nothin' to do with it."

It wasn't necessary to say more; the last lingering doubt had fled from the minds of Morgan's bunch. The hard-bitten faces ranged along the bar reflected only approval of the owl hooter's shrewdness. As the outlaws stood there, filling their glasses, a mousy-looking little man hurried in.

"What is it, Smoky?" Blue demanded.

"They're up there on the bluff . . . all three of 'em!"

"Did you hear that, boys?" Morgan grinned. "They showed up even sooner than I predicted. That makes this one on the house." He opened a fresh bottle and slid it across the bar. "Drink up! We'll stick around awhile and make some noise. We want 'em to know we're all here. A little later we'll start slippin' down the creek, one at a time. That little meadow where Ben killed the coyote will be a good place to meet."

"Who'll yuh leave to run the joint?" Ben Ruby asked.

"Smoky can handle it." Morgan turned to the little man

83

with the mousy look. "Tomorrow mornin' when Ripley and Gibbs notice how quiet things is they'll be down in a hurry. When they ask where we pulled out for, Smoky, you tell 'em Wyomin'. They'll know that's a damned lie and begin lookin' for a trail to follow." Blue's cruel mouth twitched forbiddingly. "We'll sure leave 'em one!" he growled. "Before Ripley gets to the end of it I'll change his mind for him about a thing or two!"

Down through the Painted Bluffs and across the railroad Rainbow, Grumpy, and Howie Hallett followed the trail that Blue Morgan left for them to find. Morgan was too smart to overplay it; a few faint horse tracks, the still-warm ashes of a campfire, a random shot when pursuit came too near, were enough.

When the trail struck off toward the river the three men rode harder and with eyes sharpened for an ambush. For four days this grim game of hare and hounds ran its course without arousing their suspicions, but they possessed too deep a vein of shrewdness to be fooled for long. In the blazing white cliffs and frowning bluffs of the San Blas badlands avenues of escape were not hard to find. When the quarry failed to take advantage of them Rainbow began to wonder. Doubt became certainty in his mind when he saw Blue's bunch deliberately pass up a chance to fade away and leave no clue to show where they had gone.

"Wait up!" he called out. "There's something wrong about this. If they wanted to get away they wouldn't be heading for that ridge. Suppose we swing off to the right and try to reach it by way of the bluffs. I want to prove something."

"Jumpin' Jehoshaphat, we'll be left high and dry if we go up thataway!" Grumpy protested. He knew this country. "There's a two-hundred-foot drop off them bluffs to the ridge. That's as far as we'd get. Blue will pull out on us and we'll never see him ag'in!"

"That's exactly what I want to find out!" Rainbow said thinly.

"What do you mean by that?" Howie and Grumpy asked as one man.

Ripley's scowl deepened. "I don't like to say it, but I'm afraid we've been taken in like a bunch of half-wits. They could have left us flat at least twice today. But there they are . . . waiting for us to come after them! We'll see what they make of this move."

They reached the bluffs only to find there was no way of getting down. Two hours later they were back where they had started from. A puff of smoke and the crack of a gun told them Morgan was still on the ridge.

"That tells me all I want to know," Rainbow said bitterly. "We've been at this business too long to be caught falling for stuff like this."

"By gravy, yo're right!" Grumpy raged. "We oughta be wearin' diapers, I reckon! The stinkin' ornery skunk! Puttin' us over a barrel like this! I'll bring you his ears before I'm through with him, I promise you!"

"He was shootin' for somethin'," Howie said with rare good sense. "Puttin' the hog laugh on us wasn't what he had on his mind.

"You're right!" Rainbow ground out. "They drew us down here so we'd be sure to be out of the way of something."

"It can't be the stickin' up of another silk train," Grumpy argued. "That wouldn't make sense. We know Morgan's got his whole gang with him here . . . a hundred miles from the railroad."

"And I suppose you could say they're just as far from the river as we are," Ripley picked him up. "So the Hammersley Expedition couldn't figure in it either."

"Waal, that's a fact, ain't it?"

"Suppose we forget the facts and start using our imaginations," Rainbow advised. "Maybe we better forget what passed between Brant and Morgan that night in Black Forks. I don't care how wild you think this is, it looks to me as though Blue is playing the other man's game."

Grumpy was about to dismiss the observation with the

ridicule he believed it deserved, when suddenly he straightened up in his saddle and stared at Ripley with frozen eyes. "Rainbow, you hit it! You wouldn't listen when I tried to tell you that it was the Thane girl——"

"No, Grumpy, it's not that. If Karen Thane is in danger it's from Hammersley. There's three sides to this game, each ready to knife or use one or both of the others to pull the chestnuts out of the fire. Morgan's carried us out of this fight for a few days, but he's carried himself out of it too. The thing for us to do now is to give him the slip and start looking for the boats. They must be down as far as Spirit Canyon by now. Another two days should put them in Island Park. We ought to be there before then. And something tells me the lid is going to be blown off this whole devilish business!"

Chapter Ten

*U*TAH JIM MCBRIDE, ably assisted by Brant's men, had brought the boats through Lodore with only a few minor mishaps. They were tied up now at the mouth of the Yampa River, and they had been there for two days, two days of drizzling rain that made it necessary for the members of the expedition to sleep aboard the boats.

Having arrived at this position, only a few miles above the Rocky Mountain Shortline bridge, Thaddeus Hammersley knew the time had come to dispense with McBride's services. A few words of unwarranted criticism had brought on an argument that had ended, as the professor wished, in McBride asking for his pay. By going up the Yampa a few miles it was possible to get out of the canyons and reach Silverbow.

When the guide left, Itchi went with him, his announced purpose being to send several important telegrams. The wires were far more important than Karen or the members of the expedition not in the professor's confidence had any reason to suspect. This being the first opportunity the members of the expedition had had to dispatch letters since leaving Black Forks, they took advantage of it, and the Japanese was quite willing to make his mission appear even more innocent by playing mail carrier.

When Itchi had been gone the better part of two days and a night, and the rain continued to fall, mingled anxiety and impatience took possession of the wet, miserable camp. A dozen times an hour Hammersley strode up the canyon, looking for him, his hawklike face thinner than ever.

Brant's men had made a leaky shelter of brush. They held to it, keeping apart from the others. They knew what the Japanese was waiting for at Silverbow, that a few hours after his return things would reach their climax. They had their own ideas about it, and when Brant stepped in among them Ginger Revell voiced those ideas.

"When the Jap gets back and we know everythin' is set, Brant, why don't we git rid of this half-baked perfessor and take charge of things? We can stick up a train without any help from him or this Itchi. Then whatever we git away with will be ours."

"Not yet, Ginger," Brant said positively. "We'll take things over, but not until Hammersley ain't no further use to us. He was out here a couple years ago doing some work—or pretending to. He sized up this river along the railroad until he knows it by heart. He's got the place picked out where we're going to get up to the tracks. But more important than that, he's got a spot where the stuff can be cached. He says it won't rot if it has to stay there a year."

"You mean to tell us you never got out of him where the place is?" Revell demanded suspiciously.

"That's his secret, Ginger. When the stuff is nicely tucked away it will be time enough for us to get rid of him and the Jap."

Night was settling down when Brant and Hammersley saw Itchi sloshing down the canyon. They walked out to meet him. He raised his dripping face to them in a half grin.

"Tonight," he said. "A few minutes before twelve, Doctor. It is a most favorable hour for our plans. And before daylight comes we will have the silk out of our possession."

"Excellent! Excellent!" Hammersley murmured, his eyes burning in their deep sockets. "If we leave here at ten o'clock we shall have all the time we need. . . . We have been sleeping aboard the boats. I've arranged them so that the one to be cut adrift is moored nearest to the mouth of the river. It will be a simple matter to cut the rope; the current will do the rest."

Brant's eyes narrowed in his hard face. "It's murder!" he growled. "Borelius and Darwin will never be able to keep the boat off the rocks in the dark. The first rapids will be their finish! The women will drown with them!"

The professor turned his baleful glance at him. "That's very touching, Mr. Brant!"

"If you'd listened to me this morning and let them go on ahead we'd have had 'em out of the way," the other rasped. "That would have been enough."

Hammersley showed him his contempt. "Evidently the lesson you received in Brown's Park taught you nothing. I'll remind you that I make the decisions."

Brant refused to be cowed. "I guess you made this decision a long while back," he said defiantly. "There's one person in that boat whose death will net you a fortune and keep you from being sent up for the money you've already got away with. It ain't got nothing to do with sticking up the Silk Express. It's your own private game!"

"And I accept full responsibility for it!" The professor's iron restraint seemed to desert him completely, and his voice shook with fury. "I warn you not to interfere!"

"I'm sure the warning is unnecessary, Doctor," Itchi intervened. This display of emotion secretly disgusted him. "Mr. Brant would hardly be so foolish as to do anything that would prevent us from stopping the train. It undoubtedly has occurred to him that he and his men could overpower us. But he will not be tempted by that tonight. He knows he needs us quite as much as we need him."

Having his mind read for him in this fashion only added fuel to Brant's hatred of the Japanese. He realized, however, that Itchi had stated the situation correctly.

"All right," he gave in. "Just so we understand each other. What about Potts? We'll still have him on our hands unless you cut him adrift too."

"I refuse to lose the use of two boats," Hammersley said flatly. "Nevertheless, Dr. Potts will be removed."

The black mantle of night dropped over the canyons before supper was finished. If Karen and the others whose lives now hung in the balance failed to sense the sinister tension of these hours it was only because they were so wet and miserable. Darwin and Borelius had rigged a piece of canvas over the boat, propping it up with poles. Karen and Anne Wattress were glad to return to its uncertain shelter.

Hammersley ordered the cook fire put out a few minutes later. "We'll be making an early start in the morning," he announced. "It will be a hard day, so the sooner we turn in the better."

There was sleep only for his unsuspecting victims. At nine-thirty he spoke to Itchi. "It is time. Just cut the rope."

The Japanese nodded and silently slipped down the bank. A slight tug as the blade cut through the strands of hemp was the only warning Karen and the others received that they were being cast adrift, and it was not enough to wake them.

Itchi watched the boat disappear, its speed increasing the second that the flood pouring down into Missionary Run caught it. Turning, he made his way back up the wet bank. In his eagerness he tripped over a line and fell heavily enough to awaken Ulysses Potts from his troubled slumber.

"Who's that?" the startled little man demanded excitedly.

He got no answer, but the next moment he saw that the boat which had been tied up next to his was gone. A shrill cry that would have aroused the camp had it been fast asleep broke from his lips.

"Help!" he yelled. "Dr. Hammersley, a boat is missing! It has been swept out into the current!"

Thoroughly aroused to the danger of those aboard the missing craft, Potts leaped ashore and ran to the stake to which it had been tethered. A match flared in his hand, and with a gasp of horror he saw that the rope had been cut. Behind him he heard a man getting to his feet. He whirled to find himself facing Itchi.

"*You!*" he cried accusingly. "You cut this rope and sent those people to their death! You have the knife still in your hand!"

"No, Doctor," the Japanese murmured respectfully, "it is a gun, not a knife. I am so sorry this is necessary."

Raising his pistol, he fired. With a faint, tired sigh Ulysses Potts sagged to the wet ground and lay still. Picking up the body, Itchi gently lowered it into the river.

No one ran up to ask what had happened; they knew. Even when Itchi returned to where Hammersley waited, a questioning glance and a brief, answering nod was explanation enough.

"Mr. Brant, call the men together," the professor ordered. "I have some instructions for them." In the blackness of the night his lean face was a ghastly white mask. When the men were assembled he said: "We are ready to leave. My boat will go first; the others will follow it closely. Don't let the current carry you down into Missionary Run. I want you to strike straight across to the far wall of the canyon. As soon as you reach it dump everything overboard that will lighten the boats. The night is black, but you will be able to make out the railroad bridge ahead of you. When you are within two hundred yards of it you will find where a shallow cove has been scooped out of the wall. Take your boats into it."

He repeated his instructions so there could be no doubt of what was to be done.

"When we are all in the cove," he continued, "we will pull the boats out of the water. From there we can reach the tracks in several minutes. Now does every man know what he is to do, once we get there?"

Ginger and the others responded that they did. The professor turned to Brant.

"Mr. Brant, is it necessary for you to repeat your directions to your men regarding how the express is to be handled?"

"No," was the gruff, tense answer. "You carry out your part and there won't be a hitch!"

The men took their places in the boats and cast off the lines.

"Put your oars in the water!" came Hammersley's high-pitched command. "Pull away!"

Chapter Eleven

THERE was a hand-operated semaphore just outside the door of the lonely station at Green River Bridge. It lacked nine minutes of midnight when the agent stepped out and set the signal, giving the express the green light. Listening at the open rear window, Saburo Itchi had caught the message that the man had just taken off the wire, reading it as easily as the operator. Knowing they had only a few minutes to go before the train would be there, he slipped around the corner of the tiny building and struck the operator down with the barrel of his gun.

Picking up the unconscious man, he dragged him inside, dumped him in a closet, and locked the door on him. A moment later he was back at the signal and set it at red. He knew it would tell Brant and the others, waiting up the track, that all was going well.

The wily Japanese had no intention of cutting off telegraphic communication. He knew those thin strands of wire could gain them time if he remained at the key, time that they must have to get the silk to the boats. Turning down the lamp on the operator's table, he picked up a red lantern and ran outside. The rails were humming already. Suddenly a streak of light cut through the night as the onrushing express swung around a curve.

Itchi began to wave his lantern in frantic warning. Even his iron will faltered as he saw the headlight racing toward him, speed unchecked. Suddenly he heard the brake shoes grab as the engineer, seeing that the signal was set against him, slapped on the air. With sparks flying from the screeching, protesting wheels the train ground to a breathless stop. Engine crew, conductor, and brakeman piled down, closely followed by three guards who were aboard. A warning blast of gunfire met them. Before they could put up any resistance Brant and his men, faces masked, had them covered and disarmed.

"Keep your hands up and head for the bridge!" came the sharp command. "You're going across on the footboards! Start moving!"

Itchi saw them coming and discreetly stepped back into the office. The train crew hesitated as they reached the narrow cat-walk across the bridge. A misstep would send a man plunging into the river.

"I'll give you ten seconds to get out of sight!" a harsh voice thundered. The Japanese knew it was Brant doing the talking. "When you get across keep on going!"

The men disappeared out over the river. Brant emptied his gun over their heads. He could hear them running.

"They'll be halfway across Colorado before they stop!" he yelled at Itchi as he ran back to where Revell and the others were blasting a door off a car.

Professor Hammersley had taken no actual part in the holdup, but as the car door fell he appeared out of the wet night and speeded up the work of handling the bales of raw silk and getting them down to the boats. The excitement of the moment had taken complete possession of him. With the strength that comes to the mentally unbalanced he matched the best efforts of such burly giants as Gass Labelle.

"What a pity, Mr. Brant!" he burst out wildly. "There's a million dollars here, and we could help ourselves to all of it if we only had more boats!"

Brant found the man's voice barely recognizable. He gave him a suspicious glance. "And you're the gent who called me greedy!" he mocked. "We'll take what we can and be satisfied! Suppose you climb out of here and see what the Jap is doing. We'll need another forty minutes!"

For the first time the professor took direction from Brant. Leaping to the ground, he ran to the station. Itchi was tapping out a message.

"What is it?" Hammersley demanded.

"The operator at Silverbow. He's asking if the special has passed here."

"You told him yes——"

The Nipponese shook his head. "I shall wait another five minutes. By the time Silverbow realizes that the train is lost between the river and that station we should be almost finished. I shall cut the wire then." The professor's trembling excitement had not escaped Itchi. "May I suggest that you calm yourself, Doctor?" he said smoothly. "The situation calls for your most sober judgment."

His inflexible will seemed to reach out and touch the older man and steady him. With a curt nod Hammersley returned to the opened car. "Everything is going as we planned, Mr. Brant," he said. "I am going down to the boats now. When I send up word that they are loaded as heavily as we can risk, gather your men and bring them down. It's a rocky path; the rain will wash away any sign that we used it."

"What about Itchi?"

"He'll be the last man down, and he'll make sure we haven't left anything behind that might cast suspicion on us."

The work went on feverishly, the men toiling up and down the slippery wet slope, pausing only to catch their breath. Brant, working in the car, finally growled: "That must be pretty near the end of it! The car's almost empty! What's Hammersley doing with all the stuff?"

Ginger Revell appeared at the door a moment later. "The boats are down to the gun'ls," he told them. "This'll be the last load."

"That Hammersley's orders?" Brant demanded.

"No! But we know what them boats will carry better than him! I tell you we've reached the limit, unless you want to swamp 'em!"

"All right!" Brant whipped out. "This load is the last. You oughta know what you're talking about!"

They were just getting down from the car when Itchi appeared from the direction of the station. "We shall have to be leaving," he announced without raising his voice. "I have been listening to the messages being flashed back and forth. The railroad officials suspect the truth. Just before I cut the wire I learned that a trainload of armed men had left Platte City some minutes ago. We shall have to hurry."

They found the boats dangerously low in the water. Even so, the professor flew into a rage on realizing that work had stopped. "There is some current in the Run, but there are no rapids here or in Spirit Canyon!" he sad furiously. "Order the men up again, Brant!"

Itchi appeared then, and his news put an end to the argument. A few minutes later the boats were pushed out of the cove. Silently the swift-flowing river carried them away in trackless flight.

In the course of a few miles the current lost its mad haste. The canyon walls began to recede.

"We are leaving Missionary Run," the professor reminded Itchi. "Presently the river will spread out to a width of three hundred yards." He spoke to Revell, who was handling the steering oar, cautioning him to keep close to the Utah side. "The water is deep in there and scarcely raises a ripple."

The job was only half done. The weary men discovered as much when they found themselves moving into the mouth of an unnamed creek that cut its narrow way through the wall.

"Is this the place?" Brant asked.

"Yes, Mr. Brant," the professor answered triumphantly.

"This is where we shall cache the silk. By daylight, if you were on the opposite bank or passing down the canyon, you could look up and see a curious line of tumbled rocks some hundred feet below the rim. They seem to be lodged on a wide shelf that cuts back into the wall. They are not just rocks, I assure you; they are the ruins of ancient cliff dwellings that have been there for centuries. We discovered them two summers ago and very wisely said nothing about them."

Itchi nodded approvingly. With the finding of these unknown cliff dwellings their plans for looting the Silk Express had first occurred to them.

The men raised their faces to the rain and stared above, but in the blackness of the night they could see nothing.

"If no one knows anything about the ruins it must be because they're impossible to reach," Brant argued.

"There is a way," the professor murmured. "The same way the ancient cliff dwellers used, Mr. Brant. It's a long climb but not particularly difficult. Within three hours we can accomplish our task. If you're ready I will lead the men up the hidden path."

"Wait a minute!" Brant objected. "Let me get this straight. Is this the only means of reaching the place?"

"There is no other way!" Hammersley's eyes burned with a cunning satisfaction.

"Then when we get the silk up there it will mean another expedition—boats, expense, and risk of getting it out!" Brant's voice shook with baffled rage and chagrin. The Japanese and Hammersley read him with perfect understanding.

"Don't let that trouble you, Mr. Brant," the latter advised with sharp inflection. "When the time comes to remove the silk I shall provide a way. It will be expensive, but it will not call for boats, and it will be accomplished with the minimum risk."

"That means reaching it by coming down over the rim," Samson Brant thought. He felt tricked and cheated, but he told himself if Hammersley could find a means of reaching the cliff dwellings so could he.

"All right, boys!" he told the sullen men. "Let's get started!"

As they lugged the heavy bales of silk up the long, devious trail to the cliff dwellings Ginger Revell and the other men cursed themselves, as well as Brant and the professor, for ever having engaged in this undertaking. The primitive people, who had first used this dim trace, had hacked it out of the solid rock and worn it smooth with their bare feet. Though it climbed upward by easy stages, and there were places where a man could rest his load, even big Gass Labelle's lungs were heaving when he reached the ruins.

"By gar, dat's damn stiff climb!" he gasped. "We nevaire get all dem bale up here in two, t'ree hour!"

Brant eyed the dwellings through the gloom with frank misgiving. "They look ready to cave in," he said.

"They have stood here at least five hundred years, Mr. Brant," Itchi informed him. "They are slowly crumbling into dust, but it is quite safe to enter."

He and the professor led the way into the dark interior of the communal house and pointed out where the bales were to be stored. The whirring wings of a disturbed colony of bats showered the men with dust as they put down their burdens.

"Dry in here," Brant muttered. "What did these people live on, professor?"

"Corn and some vegetables."

That means gardens," Brant told himself. "It proves they had some means of reaching the rim."

Labelle's assertion that the work could not be completed in two or three hours proved true. Even with Hammersley's goading, a leaden dawn was breaking by the time they were finished. The professor ordered that loose rock and dust be spread over the bales, against the improbable chance of someone finding his way to the ruins.

Hammersley and the Japanese exchanged an understanding

nod as they saw the men glancing across the river and taking their bearings.

"Obviously they hope to be able to find their way back here," Itchi murmured. "There is no reason why it should disturb us, but it is to be regretted that our plans to be away before daylight have miscarried."

"It is nothing," the professor informed him. Once more he was his cool, calculating self. "Our immediate concern is to run Whirlpool Canyon and wreck the boats. I had expected to wait until we were well down into Island Park to do it. There it would have been a simple matter for us to have got out unaided if the disappearance of the expedition went unnoticed. It's too late for that now. The first rocky islands we reach will have to do."

"Not on your life!" Brant flared when Hammersley outlined his changed plans. "If we're going to make it look like an' accident we'll have to do more than smash the boats! Food—everything will have to go, and we'll be left there to rot or starve to death! We ain't taking any chance like that, Hammersley!"

The men growled their agreement with him.

"It is a chance we shall have to take, Mr. Brant," the Japanese said inflexibly. "When the river spreads out in Island Park it becomes a millpond. In those quiet waters it would be impossible to contrive anything that would have the appearance of disaster. And that is vital, Mr. Brant—whatever the risk—if we are to escape suspicion. Going hungry for a day or two will be a small price to pay."

"What makes you so sure it will be only a day or two?"

"Because an intensive search will be instituted for the men who looted the Silk Express." Itchi spoke with a pitying contempt for Brant's lack of perception. "In the past you expressed the direst apprehension regarding Mr. Rainbow Ripley and Mr. Gibbs. Your anxiety was somewhat premature, as events have proven, but I can assure you the time has come when all of us must regard them with the utmost concern."

"True—absolutely!" exclaimed the professor. "We took advantage of them once, and they are not the kind to forget it. They will lead this man hunt, and they will stick with it."

"You fools!" Brant ripped out, his hard face livid with rage. "Don't start agreeing with me, now that the fat's in the fire! I warned you right along you were letting them know too much! And don't kid yourselves that you tricked 'em! That's a habit of theirs to give a man rope enough to hang himself!" He was so impressed by his own arguments that he had no further objection to being marooned on the rocky headlands at the entrance to Island Park. He spoke to his men, and they gave in too.

"Hammersley, if you're running things get going!" Brant thundered. "What a laugh it would be if we found that pair waiting for us down in the islands! Waiting with Miss Thane's body, and old Potts and the others! When this river gives up its dead you'll wish you'd listened to me! Both of you!"

Itchi's teeth gleamed white against his thick lips. "You are distressing yourself needlessly, Mr. Brant. Whirlpool Canyon has been aptly named. It does not give up its secrets. A few hours will be enough."

His complacency would have been rudely jarred had he known that at the moment Ripley, Grumpy, and Howie Hallett were putting their horses down into the rainbow-hued valley of rounded hills and painted rocks and marls that white men call Island Park.

Chapter Twelve

S EEMS LIKE we shook 'em off," Grumpy declared. He, Rainbow, and Hallett had pulled up in a grove of cottonwoods and scanned their back trail for half an hour. "Blue Morgan shore tried hard to stick with us!"

"Provin' that he had somethin' awful definite on his mind," observed Howie.

Rainbow murmured his agreement. "We may find the answer right here in Island Park." He squinted an eye at the sky. "Going to clear off. . . . I've got a little coffee left. That'll have to be the size of our breakfast."

"It'll take a man a week to work out this place," Hallett remarked, studying the panorama opening out before him as the mist began to rise. For miles the river had spread out to the dimensions of a lake, studded with rocky, heavily wooded islands. "How do you know where to start lookin'?"

"We'll have the coffee first, then start working up toward the head of the park," Rainbow said. "If the boats have come down we'll see them."

The sun came out as they moved along the bank a short while later. Before they had gone a mile Grumpy pointed to a column of smoke rising from one of the islands.

"They're here!" the little man declared. "Got a fire goin'!"

"Yeah," Rainbow said. "There's someone waving to us. It's Jim Darwin! Come on! I think we can get out there with the horses. There's only two or three feet of water in here."

"Funny we don't see the boats," Grumpy muttered as they put their ponies into the river and struck across to the island. "Must be over on the other side."

Ripley nodded but did not commit himself. Even at a distance he sensed Darwin's excitement. "Well, I see you got here!" he called out as he reached the island's sloping shore.

"By a miracle, Rainbow!" Jim's young face had a drawn, haggard look. It brought a sharp question from Ripley.

"Something wrong?"

"There's just three of us here—Karen, Anne, and myself. We lost Borelius last night. The side of our boat was crushed in, up in the Run. We were all in the water, hanging on. Borelius let go for a second. I saw a whirlpool catch him and drag him under." Darwin shook his head sadly. "There wasn't anything I could do."

"What were you doin' comin' down Whirlpool Canyon by night?" Grumpy demanded crossly.

"Wait!" Rainbow told him. "Suppose you tell us what happened, Jim. Where did you leave the others?"

"At the mouth of the Yampa. We'd been tied up there for two days. McBride had a row with Dr. Hammersley and walked out on us. Then Itchi had to hike all the way to Silverbow to send some wires and take out some letters. It had been raining, and we had been sleeping on the boats. Last night I woke up to find that we were being swept down Missionary Run. I don't know how it happened. I suppose the line broke or came loose."

"Funny they didn't notice you was gone and come after you," Grumpy observed, his voice rough with suspicion.

"I suppose they did look for us," Darwin said. "Karen is afraid they may have smashed up trying. The night was so black you couldn't see ten feet. There's a lot of current in the Run. Before we could get our oars in the rowlocks we crashed into the wall. The stern bulkhead was the only one that didn't cave in."

"Did you have your life jackets on?" Rainbow asked.

"We got them on in a hurry when we saw the boat was filling with water," Jim told him. "Borelius and I agreed that it wouldn't carry us; that the only thing we could do was to go overboard and hang on as long as the boat stayed afloat. It was a terrible experience! We must have been in the water six hours!" He looked around him wearily and found a place to sit down. "Poor Borelius! I can't help thinking he sacrificed himself to save us. He seemed to shove the boat away from him."

"Jim, whereabouts on the Yampa were you tied up?" Rainbow asked. He was as sure as Grumpy that the boat had been set adrift at Hammersley's order.

"Why, at the mouth of the river," Darwin answered.

Ripley nodded. "That's what I thought! It was asking for something like this. Where is the boat now?"

"At the head of the island, I just finished getting out a

few things and spreading them on the beach to dry. Anne's sketchbook and Karen's camera—that's about all."

"Did you look at the rope?"

"No, I didn't."

"I'd like to see it," said Rainbow. "Come on."

A glance at the severed line left no doubt that it had been cut. Darwin's mouth tightened grimly.

"Rainbow, is that what you meant when you warned me not to trust Dr. Hammersley and Itchi?"

"It's part of what I meant. I knew an attempt would be made to separate the innocent members from the expedition and leave it in the hands of those who are using it as a clever cover-up for their game. When you were set adrift only Dr. Potts was left to bother them. I predict that we'll never see him alive again."

Darwin stared at him aghast. "I can't believe what you are telling me! I know Dr. Hammersley is eccentric, but surely he would never lend himself to anything like this. It was Brant I feared——"

"He's a crook, but not half as dangerous as Hammersley and the Jap. They've got the brains; brains enough to be ruthless and cunning." Rainbow's eyes were sharp and sober. "I knew Karen was in danger, but I thought you and Borelius and McBride would be able to stop any move that was made against her. If I hadn't thought so I wouldn't have left you in Brown's Park, though Grumpy and I had reasons for leaving." He turned to his partner to find the latter regarding him with grimly triumphant eyes. "You called the turn this time."

"I said if I was only a third right it was righter than I wanted to be," the little man reminded him. "I reckon we can rule out Morgan an' Brant an' charge this up to the professor. . . . That girl ain't safe for a minute with that old wolf on the loose! An' the worst of it is that you can't tell her."

"I don't want her to know," said Rainbow. "She wouldn't believe it anyhow. But I can convince you in a hurry, Jim."

It did not take him long to acquaint Darwin with the facts

101

and conclusions that he and Grumpy had arrived at. It left the young scientist convinced and speechless for a minute.

"It takes my breath away," he managed finally. "I can look back now and recall a dozen things that should have warned me what we were up against." He shook his head in bitter self-reproach. "I was sound asleep! I didn't even suspect there was anything wrong about that accident at Ashley Falls. Rainbow, what first made you suspicious of the expedition?"

"Hammersley trying to sign us up. It didn't make sense; what was there we could do for him? I got wise in a hurry when Grumpy spotted Ginger Revell and I began to get the real answer when I saw the size and shape of the boats you were to use. I wouldn't have tumbled if they had been designed by some half-wit who had never laid eyes on this river. But Hammersley was out here a couple of years ago, and before that he was down on the lower Colorado where things really get tough. I refused to believe he was crazy enough to think for one minute that he could make the descent in boats like those. It gave me the idea that the boats were intended for some other purpose than the one he was giving out."

"Look out, Rip!" Howie warned before Rainbow could say more. "Here comes the girl."

"I thought I heard voices," Karen called to them, picking her way down the rocky ledge to the beach. "I'm so glad you're here, Rainbow! I told Jim we could expect you. I presume he's been telling you what happened." She had slept for an hour and it seemed to have refreshed her. "It was a terrifying experience. We didn't know we were down among the islands until we felt our feet touching bottom in the shallow water."

"I'm glad you came this far," Rainbow told her. "It'll be easy to get you out. The sooner we do it the better. The nearest place is Dan Priest's ranch. He'll be glad to take you in."

"But Uncle and the others?" Karen protested. "We can't leave them! They need help more than we!"

"I doubt it," said Rainbow. Karen's concern for Professor Hammersley and her blind faith in the man tested his patience. "It seems improbable that all of their boats could have met disaster. In any event we're taking you and Miss Wattress to the ranch before we start looking for them." He turned to Hallett. "I want you to stay here, Howie, and watch this stuff. We won't be able to take anything out with us. You can be on the lookout for the other boats. Grump and I will come back or send one of Dan's men down with horse and grub."

Karen's sharp cry of disappointment swung him around. She had just discovered that her negatives had been lost. "It's selfish, I suppose, even to think of the negatives when we have so much to be thankful for, but they were priceless to me."

"I know," Darwin told her, "but we're alive, Karen; that's the important thing!" He put a protective arm about her and a sharp twinge of envy ran through Rainbow. "You've kept your chin up so far. Don't let this get you down. You call Anne, and we'll get started."

Anne Wattress was forty, but she had withstood the ordeal better than Karen. She had a cheerful smile for Grumpy. "I told you I had starved for my art in Europe fifteen years ago," she said with a laugh, "but I refuse to drown for it." She picked up her sketchbook. "Soaked!" she declared. "It will be a record of the trip though. How far is it to this ranch, Grumpy?"

" 'Bout twelve miles. We can ride double."

"Cheer up, Karen!" Anne said. "We have only twelve miles to go. Breakfast will be late this morning, but there will be breakfast—I hope!" Her lively comment was meant to lift the girl's spirits, and it was not without effect.

Karen rode with Rainbow. Holding the horses to a walk, they climbed out of Island Park and headed north across the high plateau for Dan Priest's Cross Keys Ranch.

"Jim tells me that when McBride left you Itchi went out with him," he said after a long silence.

"Yes, to a place called Silverbell or Silverbow."

103

"Silverbow. . . . Karen, do you remember how long Itchi was gone?"

"He left one morning and was back at dark the next day——"

"Thirty-six hours," Ripley murmured thoughtfully. "It's not over twelve miles each way. He must have waited there for an answer to his telegram."

"I believe he said he did," she agreed.

"And a few hours later you found yourself being carried down Missionary Run."

"Why, yes." Karen caught a note of misgiving in his clipped words. "Why do you ask about Itchi, Rainbow?"

"Just curious," was his evasive answer. He had only been dropping the missing pieces of this puzzle into place. There was no doubt left in his mind regarding Saburo Itchi's purpose in going to Silverbow or of the answer the Japanese had received to his telegram.

Rainbow's reply had not satisfied Karen. "You're not being frank with me," she said accusingly. "You're holding back something, Rainbow."

"It isn't worth worrying about," he endeavored to reassure her. "I don't like Itchi, and that's the size of it." He was glad to have Darwin ride up beside them.

"That must be the house there under the bluff," Jim observed. "Quite a ranch this man's got here."

"You'll be comfortable for a few days. Dan and his wife will be glad to have you; they don't see much company."

Dan Priest stepped out on the gallery as they rode into the yard. He didn't try to hide his surprise at seeing Rainbow and Grumpy there.

"Waal!" he declared. "I didn't figger I'd be seein' you fellas today! I know yo're workin' for the railroad. Ain't yuh heard the news?"

"Holdup?" Grumpy demanded instantly.

"Yeah! One of them silk expresses, at Green River Bridge last night. They say some gang got away with a big bag of stuff. Quarter of a million or thereabouts! What's the matter, Rainbow? Yuh don't act surprised."

"No, Dan, I was all set for this. Just came a little sooner than I expected." Ripley gave Grumpy and Darwin a warning glance. He knew he had to talk fast if Karen was to be spared. "Sounds like Blue's work. We've been chasing him for a week. What time last night did it happen, Dan?"

" 'Bout midnight. I hear they got away without leavin' a trace of which way they went. The rain helped 'em. Won't you folks git down? I'd like to have yuh come in." He stepped to the door. "Emmy!" he called to his wife. "Come out! We got company!"

Rainbow helped Karen down. She immediately turned to Priest. "Is there any word about the Hammersley Expedition?"

"Why, yuh mean them folks that are goin' down the river, ma'am?"

"Yes."

"No, I ain't heard anyone say nuthin'. Down in them canyons they're purty well cut off from everythin'. Them folks friends of yores, ma'am?"

"Dan, let me explain," Ripley spoke up. "These people are members of the expedition. This is Miss Thane and Miss Wattress and Professor Darwin. They had a serious accident. We found them in Island Park this morning and I brought them here. I knew you and the missus wouldn't mind taking them in."

"Why, no, not at all!" the old cowman declared. "Emmy and me will be glad to have yuh."

The question in Karen's mind had not been answered, and she tried again. "Mr. Priest, the last we saw of Professor Hammersley and the others was at the Yampa River, a few hours before the robbery. It was so near the bridge. Could they have been attacked by those outlaws?"

"Why, no!" Dan said emphatically. "If it was Blue's bunch that did the job they got away from the river in a hurry."

The answer seemed to satisfy the girl. Rainbow exchanged another anxious glance with Grumpy and Darwin. Clearer than ever before, he realized how hard it was going to be on her when she realized the truth about her uncle.

Mrs. Priest, a little gray-haired woman with a merry laugh, appeared in the doorway. "Dan, why didn't yuh ask the ladies in?" she said reprovingly. "Yuh knew I was bakin' and couldn't come a-runnin'!"

Rainbow turned from introducing her to her unexpected guests to tell Karen that he was leaving Darwin there with her and Miss Wattress.

"Grumpy and I will be back tomorrow or the day following," he promised. "We'll try to find some kind of a boat in Vernal and bring it down by wagon. If Howie hasn't seen anything of the professor's party in the meantime we'll start searching for them. "You step in with Mrs. Priest now; I want to have a few words with Dan and arrange to have him send one of his boys to the island. I don't want you to worry; everything will be all right."

Karen raised her level eyes to him. "Thank you for all you've done, Rainbow," she murmured.

Priest walked the partners and Darwin across the yard to his blacksmith shop. "Of course . . . of course!" he said in answer to Rainbow's request that he send a puncher down to Island Park. "But that ain't what yuh was bendin' over backward to keep them wimmen from hearin'. I saw yuh freeze up the second I mentioned the robbery."

"Naturally," Ripley said flatly. He didn't intend to have this go any further. "After being swept down the river for fifteen to twenty miles, clinging to a sinking boat, I didn't figure the women were in any condition for more worry and excitement; Darwin can tell you about that. We're pulling away for the bridge as fast as we can get there. Is there anything else you know about the holdup?"

"No. One of the boys came back from town this mornin' with the news, jest as I gave it to yuh."

"O.K., Dan! If you'll get us a little grain for the horses we'll be on our way."

Darwin could hardly wait until they were alone to voice his

racing thoughts. "They robbed that train just as the two of you predicted they would!" he got out breathlessly. "They've got the silk on the boats and are running down the canyons with it!"

"That seems to be the answer," Rainbow muttered. "Get this, Jim: don't let a word slip to Dan about it! He'll know soon enough. And don't let Karen out of your sight. If you have to use your gun on those sidewinders don't hesitate!"

"I won't," Jim promised grimly. "You know what Karen means to me."

Ripley nodded soberly and wheeled away. "Get up the horses!" he told Grumpy. "Here's Dan with the oats!"

He took the small bag of feed and draped it over his saddle horn. "So long!" he said, waving.

They had better than twenty miles of riding ahead of them and they gave themselves to it with a will. An hour later they were cutting through the Painted Bluffs.

"You don't have much to say." Grumpy's tone had a tense, anxious note. "You wonderin' where we stand?"

"Not for a minute!" answered Rainbow. "We've got this thing cracked wide open. We can put our finger on every man involved in the robbery. Soon as we find out where Hammersley has cached the silk we'll be ready for a house cleaning; and we'll include Blue and his gang when we start to close in."

"It sounds promisin'," the doughty little man muttered uneasily. "I hope Tom Moran feels that way about it. We'll find him and a bunch of bigwigs waitin' for us at the bridge."

"I'm ready for 'em," Rainbow answered grimly.

Chapter Thirteen

T HE PARTNERS found a small crowd of men milling around outside the tiny station at Green River Bridge.

"There's Vinson and Joe Brothers," Grumpy pointed out. "I reckon that means Asa Sharp is here."

They were just stepping down from their saddles when a dumpy, pink-cheeked man with iron-gray hair put his head out the door. It was Asa Sharp, U. S. marshal for northern Utah. He recognized them at once.

"So you're here!" he called out. "Wondering where you were! Come on in!" He turned and they heard him say: "Ripley and Gibbs are here now, Moran. We'll see what they've got to say."

Tom Moran's greeting was decidedly less enthusiastic than it had been in Platte City a few weeks back. "I guess I expected too much of you," he said frankly. "I had the feeling that nothing like this could happen to us with you fellows on the job. Do you know anything about this robbery?"

Rainbow asked the operator to step outside. "We know all about it, Tom," he answered as soon as they were alone.

Sharp sat up stiffly. "Ripley, do you mean that?" he asked pointedly.

"You've known me a long time, Asa," was Rainbow's reply. "You ought to have a pretty good idea by now whether I can be depended on to mean what I say or not. That goes for my partner, too."

"Well, if you know something let's have it!" Moran broke in. "Garner has a dozen men out and hasn't turned up a thing!"

"I haven't got anywhere either," admitted the marshal. "You're acquainted with the sheriff, so you know we can't expect anything in that direction. Moran tells me you located Blue Morgan in this country. Naturally I wondered if——"

"You're wrong, Asa," Ripley cut him off. "Blue didn't have anything to do with this—at least not directly. As late as six o'clock last evening he and the bunch that's stringing along with him—Wild Bill Williams, Ben Ruby, and seven or eight others—were way down among the chalk cliffs of the San Blas Plateau. I know because we were there playing hide and seek with 'em."

108

"An' we traded a few shots with 'em durin' the night," Grumpy put in. "At daylight they was still as far south as Island Park."

"Let's get down to brass tacks and stop this beating around the bush!" Moran burst out impatiently. "Do you realize, Rainbow, that over two hundred thousand dollars' worth of silk was taken off that train?"

"So I understand," was the calm answer. "I'm here to put all the cards on the table, Tom, but I'm not going to be hurried. I could give you the names of the men responsible for this holdup; but don't get the idea that there's going to be any arrests made tomorrow or the day after. I think I can guarantee you that the silk will be recovered and that there'll be a wholesale roundup of crooks and outlaws that will clean up this country for a long time to come. I warn you there's a couple strings to that promise. You've got to agree to keep Pat Garner and his railroad detectives out of our way, and Asa here will have to agree to hold off and not do anything until we're ready to call him in. I know if you two pass me your word you'll keep it."

"Why, that's preposterous, Ripley!" exclaimed Sharp. "You can't expect the railroad company or me to put our heads into a bag like that!"

"It may sound preposterous," Rainbow acknowledged. "I'm asking you to go it blind, but there isn't any other way. Before I say any more I've got to know where Grumpy and I stand. I've a personal interest in cleaning out this nest of blacklegs, and I'm not going to have our play ruined by anyone's meddling. I say that with all respect to you, Asa; you're a good man, and we're going to need you. In fact, we'd be licked without you. But that badge you're wearing would be a handicap right now."

The marshal puffed out his pink cheeks until his face was as round as an apple as he sat there deliberating with himself. "Well," he said at last, "I've never known you to overstate yourself, Rainbow. I realize there's some steps I couldn't take that you could. How much time would you want?"

"I'll leave that to you."

"All right! If the railroad company is willing to play it your way I'll do the same. How about it, Tom?"

"That doesn't leave me anything to say but yes," Moran declared. "I wished a job on you boys in the first place that you didn't want; I won't sell you short now. Let's hear what you've got to say."

"I'll go the long way and begin with the freight wreck at Split Mountain," said Rainbow. When he got as far as the killing of Chink Johnson and the absolute identification of the woolen samples Tom Moran popped out of his chair excitedly.

"Great guns, man, will you tell me why you arrested Jackson when you had these facts in your possession? You knew he couldn't have had anything to do with the wrecking of that train!"

"If it's a lawsuit you're worryin' about, forget it," Grumpy advised. "We got enough on old Yampa to make him sit up and say please."

"But that still doesn't answer my question," Moran insisted. "Why did you do it?"

"So Blue would open up a little—which he did," answered Rainbow. "We followed him to Black Forks and got an earful."

Beginning with the meeting between Brant and Morgan, Rainbow put his amazing story of intrigue and cross-purposes together piece by piece until Sharp and Tom Moran could only sit there amazed and stunned.

"Now that the silk is out of the possession of the railroad company," Rainbow continued, "you can depend on it that Morgan will go after it stronger than ever. Brant will know where it is cached, and he and his gang will try to make off with it too."

"An' Hammersley an' the Jap will do their dangdest to double-cross both of 'em," Grumpy averred solemnly. "There'll be gun smoke over that silk, an' plenty of it!"

Ripley addressed himself to the marshal. "I guess you understand now what I meant when I said your badge would stop you from being any help to us just now. We've got to let those wolves get to fighting among themselves, then they'll lead us to the cache. Island Park would be the easiest place to hide the silk. That's a good reason why it probably won't be found there."

"That silk will be too hot to handle for a time," the marshal declared.

"Hammersley and the Jap have brains enough to know that," said Rainbow. "They won't touch it for months. But Blue and Samson Brant are just crooks; they won't wait if they get their fingers on it. We won't wait either. Just as soon as we locate the stuff we'll send for you, and it will be your party the rest of the way."

"He's right, Tom," Sharp advised Moran. "It would be a mistake to make any attempt to take that crowd into custody now."

"I agree with you," was the railroad man's unhesitating answer. "A load has been taken off my shoulders, I can tell you, Rainbow! You and Grumpy have done a great job so far. I'll go all the way with you. There won't be any question of how much time you can have. What will be your first move?"

"I'm going to try to find some sort of a boat in Vernal and lug it down to Island Park and start looking for Hammersley," replied Rainbow. "In the meantime a bluff has got to be made at scouring the country for the supposed gang that stuck up the train. You could handle that, Asa. Just don't get too far down in the Painted Bluffs. Do most of your looking north of the railroad. Then drift out of the country as though you had picked up a clue somewhere else. I don't want Blue to get the idea that you're watching him. Give him plenty of rope."

"All right," Sharp agreed. "After I leave Vernal in a day or two I'll move over to Mormon Valley and stay there until you get word to me."

"There's always a freight engine in the yard at Mormon

111

Valley," Moran put in. "We'll get you back here in a hurry when you're needed."

The marshal asked a question or two. Finally he said: "Where are you going to make your headquarters, Ripley?"

"Priest's ranch—at least for the present. But I don't want you to try to get in touch——"

"I'm only asking so I'll know where to start looking if you and Gibbs turn up missing," Sharp said quickly. "You're sticking your heads into a hornet's nest, and there's no point in fooling ourselves about it."

"Not for a minute," Rainbow agreed. "I'd like to take a look along the river here for a few yards and see just how they got the stuff down to the boats. I don't want an audience."

"I'll pull this crowd away from here," the marshal offered. "If we haven't any more to say I can start swinging through the bluffs."

Ten minutes later only Moran and the operator were left at the bridge with the partners. Rainbow questioned the operator, but the man had little to tell him.

"I can get you over to Vernal," Moran suggested. "It would save you an hour or two."

"Don't bother," Ripley told him. "We'll just have a look around and be on our way."

He and Grumpy had no difficulty in finding a path down the slope to the river. They could find no evidence that it had been used until the little one discovered a smudge of green paint on a rock at the water's edge.

"That's enough!" Grumpy rasped. "The paint's the same color as the boats. It rubbed off when they were tied up here."

"I guess that explains it," agreed Ripley. "The evidence is piling up."

They left the river behind them and followed the railroad around Split Mountain. By late afternoon they had a flat-bottomed duckboat loaded on a light wagon and were ready to strike south from Vernal.

"Before we leave we're going to drop around to the jail

and have a little talk with Yampa," Rainbow told his partner. "His hearing is coming up tomorrow. I'm not only going to tell him we won't appear against him, but see if he can't be of some use to us."

When old Yampa had been told why he was in jail he cackled inarticulately in his rage.

"Oh, stop your rantin'!" Grumpy burst out impatiently. "You got a score to settle with Blue, an' this was one way of doin' it."

Ripley finally succeeded in making the old man see it. "You'll never get your place back until Blue has been put on the shelf again," he told Yampa. "If you've got a lick of sense you'll string along with us."

"Waal, what yuh want me to do?"

"I want you to watch Morgan. If something turns up that we ought to know look for us down around Dan Priest's ranch or in the bluffs along the river between the railroad and Island Park. You know every gopher hole in that country; it shouldn't be any trick for you to find us."

Yampa wiped his tobacco-stained mouth with the back of his hand. "Aw right!" he agreed. "Fix me up with a little money an' I'll go yuh!"

Realizing that if the man was to be of any real value to them he had to be given some idea of where Morgan, Brant, and Hammersley stood in this game of cross-purposes left Rainbow no choice but to tell Yampa the whole story.

"I know Hammersley and that Jap perfessor," Yampa said to their surprise. "I did some freightin' fer 'em when they was out here two, three summers ago."

Leaving town half an hour later Grumpy did not hesitate to express his doubts about the step Ripley had taken. "That ole renegade may upset the apple cart for us. He's with you today an' agin' you tomorrow."

"He hates Morgan," Ripley argued. "That's what I'm counting on."

Knowing it would be long after midnight before they could

reach the ranch, they decided to swing wide of it and go on to Island Park without stopping. Spreading a blanket in the boat, they took turns sleeping, and when morning broke they were in sight of their destination.

The creaking of the wagon announced their approach to Howie. He was still camped where they had left him. Recognizing them, he put the coffeepot on the fire and by the time they had got the boat in the water and turned the horses out to graze he had breakfast ready.

"I ain't seen nothin' of 'em," he said without waiting for the question. "I've had the place to myself since the boy from the ranch left."

"Well, that don't sound so good," Grumpy muttered. "Mebbe we was a little previous in thinkin' we was about ready to nail their hides to the barn door."

Rainbow, however, refused to take that pessimistic view. "They're in here somewhere," he declared. "We'll have a bite to eat and start looking."

Two men were a load for the light duckboat, so Hallett had to be left behind.

"I'll do the rowing," Ripley announced. "You sit in back, Grumpy, and keep your rifle in your hands. If we stumble onto them before they've rubbed out all traces of what they've been up to they'll cut us down without thinking twice about it."

Scanning each succeeding island with enormous care before venturing within gun range, and then working around it, took time. By noon they were ready to agree with Howie that it would take a week to whip out the park thoroughly. Failure to draw a shot or see anyone did not make them careless. It was in their minds that death lurked here, and establishing that one island was deserted and innocent was no guarantee that the next would not bring a blast of bushwhack lead.

When they spoke they lowered their voices against the chance of the sound carrying, and Rainbow raised and dipped the oars in silent, measured strokes. But only the whir of wings as their approach disturbed the flocks of ducks and the

114

kingfishers that were always in sight broke the stillness of the long, drowsing day.

"We're purty close to the head of the park," Grumpy observed as evening began to fall. His tone was uneasy and tense. "Seems like we should be seein' or hearin' somethin' of 'em by now."

Rainbow nodded. He had begun to share the other's growing sense of failure.

"Has it occurred to you that it's just as easy to get out of Island Park in the direction of Colorado as by the way we come in?" the little man demanded in a hoarse, croaking whisper.

"That's true, but——"

"Be a nice kettle of fish if they'd loaded that stuff on wagons and left the river!"

"You don't find wagons waiting like that, Grumpy." Rainbow's tone was equally grave. "Hammersley could have arranged for them, but that would mean letting more greedy hands in on his secret and too many know already. We'll head back for camp; we've done all we can for today."

They were smoking an after-breakfast cigarette the following morning when Howie suddenly sat up erect. "There goes what's left of Darwin's boat!" he exclaimed. "The river must have risen a little durin' the night and put it afloat. If you want it for any reason we better go after it quick!"

"We don't need it——" Ripley started to say, only to check himself abruptly. "Darwin's boat is still there on the beach! That's another boat!" He got to his feet hurriedly. "Come on!" he ordered the little man. "I want to have a look at that hulk!"

They got hold of the drifting boat and towed it ashore, bottom up. Weeds clung to it, proof enough that it had come some distance. All three bulkheads had been split open.

"What do you make of it?" Grumpy asked when they had the battered craft drawn up out of the water. "Don't look to me like any rock stove her in thataway!"

"Nor to me," Rainbow seconded. "An ax was used on this

115

boat. There's the mark of the blade." He opened the compartments. "Nothin' in 'em," he muttered. "Stripped clean!"

Grumpy shook his gnarled head gravely. "It's what I was afraid of! They wouldn't smash the boats if they was of any further use to 'em."

"That's the way it looks to me too," Howie declared. "If they smashed one boat the chances are they smashed 'em all."

"That doesn't follow," argued Rainbow. "I can't believe they'd leave themselves high and dry without a chance of getting out."

"Wouldn't you?" Grumpy whipped out. "Well, take a squint over where we left the wagon! Ain't that another boat driftin' down, bottom up?"

Ripley could only agree that it was.

"If those boats had been wrecked down in the park they wouldn't be driftin' around over here," Hallett told him. "You know that, Rip. I'm afraid the two of you have been lookin' in the wrong place for your men."

"I'm wondering!"

"So am I!" Grumpy growled. "You talked mighty convincin' to Sharp and Moran, but it begins to appear that some of them aces we thought we was holdin' is just deuces. If we ever find Hammersley an' his litter of reptiles it won't be in Island Park."

Rainbow stood there, tall, resolute, his lips tightly clamped together. "Wherever they are we're going after them. That's my answer. We'll see what we can find in Whirlpool Canyon."

"Great Christopher!" the fiery little man exploded. "We can't put that cardboard thing you call a boat into that canyon!"

"Maybe we can't," was the flinty answer. "But we'll try!"

Chapter Fourteen

RETURNING SOON AFTER DAYLIGHT to the island where darkness had stopped them, Rainbow and Grumpy continued their search for Hammersley and the missing men, wary and alert to their danger. By ten o'clock they reached the head of the park. Between them and the mouth of Whirlpool Canyon only two or three rocky islets raised their barren heads.

Ripley struck out for them, bending his back against the increasing tug of the current. They were still about half a mile away when Grumpy called his attention to what seemed to be a signal of distress flying above one of the headlands.

"They're there!" Rainbow declared, shading his eyes with his hand. "They've got an oar stuck up with a shirt fastened to it! Off there to the left of them is another boat piled up on the rocks with its back broken!"

"I see it," growled Grumpy. "If you didn't know better you'd think they had been washed up there and had a bad accident. They shore made it look real!"

Rainbow nodded. "They must have been here close to sixty hours without food. They'll have a story to tell us, and we'll have to pretend to swallow it. We can be sure of one thing, though."

"Well?"

"That the silk is cached somewhere between here and the bridge—not in the park."

The men on the rock were waving by now. In a few minutes Rainbow and Grumpy were able to identify them.

"Thank heavens you found us, Ripley!" the professor called across the water. "We thought we were going to starve to death here!"

Hammersley had a wild, disheveled look, but he had plainly withstood the self-enforced fast better than Brant and his men.

"We picked up a couple of your boats and knew you were in trouble," Rainbow answered him.

Hammersley was ready with a harrowing tale of disaster, claiming that when the boat containing Karen and the others had broken away at the Yampa they had immediately started down Missionary Run, looking for it. Without the services of a guide, in the blackness of the rain-swept night they had wrecked one boat after another in Spirit and Whirlpool Canyons.

"When we crashed into this island we barely had the strength left to crawl out of the water." He sighed regretfully. "It was all for nothing! We failed to find a trace of my ward and those who were in her boat."

"I can relieve you on that point," Rainbow said, watching Hammersley closely. "We found them. They're all right—all except Professor Borelius. He was drowned."

Hammersley's hooded eyes narrowed as he struggled to dissemble his dismay. Itchi came to his rescue hurriedly.

"What good news that three were saved, Doctor!" he exclaimed with more feeling than usual. "We have so much to be thankful for."

"How true!" the professor murmured, drawing in his breath with a gasping catch. "But Borelius—he was such an able man!"

"So was Professor Potts," Rainbow remarked almost too pointedly. "I suppose he was lost too."

"Yes, he was no match for the river," Itchi answered. "He was so frail. I had a great admiration for Dr. Potts. He was a thorough scientist. By what stroke of good fortune do you and Mr. Gibbs happen to be here, Mr. Ripley?"

"We're looking for the gang that robbed the Silk Express at Green River Bridge three nights ago. We have some reason to believe they came this way." Rainbow could feel Brant and the others stiffen. Only the Japanese was equal to the moment.

"Three nights ago, Mr. Ripley?" he questioned. "That explains the shots Mr. Brant heard. We must have been going down the Run the very moment of the robbery."

"I guess that was it," Brant agreed. "I always thought those silk trains were pretty well guarded. I don't suppose the thieves got away with much."

"Two hundred thousand dollars' worth or more. That much raw silk takes some hiding. There isn't any place along the river that would do unless it's Island Park."

Hammersley was quick to agree. "From my knowledge of these canyons I would say the park is a promising place to look. But to return to our own predicament, Mr. Ripley. What can be done about removing us from this island?"

"We'll take you off, Professor, if the boat will carry three. The others have their life jackets. They'll have to take to the water and let the current carry them down into the park. They can wade out then."

They followed this plan and got Hammersley back to where they had left the wagon.

"You'll be going into Vernal," Rainbow told him, "so you might as well make use of the team. There're a few things from Darwin's boat that you can take along. In a few days I suppose you will be returning to the East."

"Oh, no!" the professor exclaimed vehemently. "I do not accept defeat so easily, Mr. Ripley! The expedition will go on. We've lost everything, but I shall telegraph for new equipment—new boats, new instruments. It may take five or six weeks before we can continue, but I shall establish a camp here close to the river and do some research while we are waiting. I owe it to the memory of the men who have lost their lives in this undertaking to finish it with glory."

Rainbow had no difficulty in understanding the man's real purpose in remaining in the country. He knew Grumpy was in no doubt about it either.

Before the others began to arrive Rainbow rowed over to Howie and helped put the camera and the other things in the boat.

"I want you to take this bunch as far as the ranch," he told

119

Howie. "Hammersley can follow the road into town from there. You stay with Dan until we show up."

An hour later Grumpy heaved a sigh of relief as he watched the wagon disappear over the hills. "Of all the lyin', snake-tongued guff I ever listened to, that takes the cake!" he snorted. "I'd like to stick a pitchfork in their gizzards and turn it around plenty! It was pretty near too much for you too. I thought you was goin' to bust out there once and tell 'em off to their teeth."

"I was tempted to," Rainbow muttered bitterly. "Maybe I said too much as it was. I caught a flicker of something in the Jap's eyes that made me ask myself just who was fooling who."

"Meanin' that they figger we know the real inside on the robbery?"

"Yeah."

The little one shook his head with deep conviction. "I don't believe that for a minute! They ain't that all-fired cute! Would they be willin' to pull out for town and leave us behind to go rootin' around for that cached stuff if they thought we was wise to everythin'? They would've kept someone here with us."

"Maybe the silk is so well hidden that they don't care how much looking we do," Rainbow countered. "And we've only got their word that they're going all the way to Vernal. I suspect Hammersley and Itchi may change their minds about that before they reach Dan's place. Certainly we're going to get up on the bluffs and see what they do. If some of them turn back I want to know it."

By the time they had climbed high enough to command a view of the plateau that led to the Cross Keys the wagon was halfway to the ranch. They watched it until only a tiny moving cloud of dust marked its progress.

"Well, I reckon that's just the same as tellin' us to go ahead an' look our eyes out," Grumpy averred. "Suppose we do! If we buckle down to it we oughta be able to work this side

120

of the river pretty careful all the way up into Spirit Canyon in two or three days."

They turned their horses back to the edge of the rim, riding so close to the very lip of the wall that it was often possible for them to scan the rocks below without leaving the saddle. Where the country was too broken for their mounts they crawled out on their bellies and studied the wall for signs of an opening or possible hiding place.

"Don't seem you could hide a canary along here," remarked Grumpy after they had been at their job for an hour. "Mebbe we're lookin' on the wrong side of the river."

"No, they couldn't have worked the boats in close enough over there," Ripley returned. "You can see how the wall shelves out. If we don't have any luck for a day or two we can take a tip on where to look when Hammersley sets up his camp. He won't pitch it too far from the thing he intends to stay here and protect. This talk of continuing down the Colorado is just a blind."

"Shore! That didn't fool nobody. If he's goin' to stick it out for two months, as he says, the girl oughta be safe fer a while."

"Yeah? How do you figure that?"

"Well, he's got two irons in the fire, ain't he? The silk is the hottest one. He'll get that off his mind first."

"I hope you're right," Rainbow muttered apprehensively as they moved on.

During the afternoon Grumpy discovered a means of getting down the wall to the river. It took hours and produced nothing. The next morning, moving into Spirit Canyon, they repeated that performance with the same result.

"It's discouraging," Rainbow admitted, "but this is the only way we can cover the ground. We've got grub enough to hold us for a day or two more."

"What about the hosses?" Grumpy asked. "A handful of grain apiece is about all we got for 'em."

"They're not doing anything. In miles, we haven't come

121

over ten or eleven since we started out. They need water more than feed."

And unrelaxing awareness of the dangerous nature of their position had settled on them and every ridge and fold of rock got their careful attention. It still left them an easy target, sky-lined as they often were for minutes at a time. This feeling of impending danger grew on them as the day advanced.

Just before the light failed they reached the little spring-fed creek from the mouth of which Hammersley had led the ascent to the cliff dwellings. They could see the tiny stream splashing down through a narrow fissure in the wall and finally flowing into the river.

"We'd have to go down on ropes to make it," declared Grumpy after a long scrutiny on the gorge. "Don't seem to be any use o' tryin' it; nuthin' but hard black granite down there without so much as a crack in it."

"We'll go back a few yards and camp," Ripley told him. "There's water and a little grass here."

They were standing on the rock roof of the cliff dwellings, but the wall cut back so far that there was no indication of the bench on which the ancient buildings had been erected, a fact that doubtless had appealed to the primitive, unwarlike builders.

"Funny there should be soil up here—three or four acres of it," Grumpy mused as they sat around after supper. "I suppose Hammersley could tell us the answer. I heard Dr. Potts sayin' one day that some of them old tribes that once lived along these rivers used to carry earth in baskets—sometimes as much as ten miles—to make a garden where they could be protected from their enemies and grow some corn."

Without realizing it Grumpy had supplied the correct answer to his question. Hammersley and Itchi had found this prehistoric garden and recognized it for what it was and after a week's searching had found the entrance to the stairs of rock that led down through the cliff to the houses. A foot of earth covered the slab of stone that concealed the hidden passage. They had carefully replaced it after their investigations, and

122

they were correct in believing that no living man shared their secret.

Seen in the bright light of early morning the narrow gorge appeared less promising than ever, and the partners decided against attempting to descend it. Ahead of them the rim became a forbidding mass of broken, crumbling rock that made any approach to the edge so dangerous that Rainbow refused to let Grumpy take a chance on it until the latter consented to having a rope tied around his middle.

They kept at it for hours, leaving the rim when it was impossible to do otherwise and striking back to the river when chance offered.

"It's no use, Rainbow," Grumpy gave in at last. "There's so much current down there now that they couldn't have held a boat long enough to unload it even if they'd had a warehouse waitin' to shove the stuff into."

Ripley grimly accepted the other's decision. "We'll give it up for now and see if Brant won't lead us to it. If we cut back through the Painted Bluffs we ought to be at the ranch before sunset. Let's be moving!"

They had gone only a mile when Grumpy reached for his rifle in a hurry. "Over there behind that nest o' boulders!" he whispered. "I saw him pull his head in!"

"Hold off thar, yuh little spit cat!" came a shrill command. "Don't go slappin' lead at me!"

"It's Yampa" Rainbow warned. "Put your gun down!"

"You'll get your adenoids operated on if you play them Injun tricks with me," Grumpy growled at the old man as the latter stepped out to meet them. "What's on your mind?"

"Boys, I got news for yuh!" Yampa cackled importantly. "Perfessor Hammersley and the Jap showed up at Ute Crossin' an' they palavered with Blue fer an hour! See what yuh make o' that!"

"Make of it?" Grumpy snorted. "It's as plain as the nose on your face! Hammersley and Itchi have put the real double-cross on Brant!"

"Selling him out all right," Rainbow confirmed. "It will be one gang fighting the other now, and the more of them that are killed off the better Hammersley will like it."

It was a startling development, though Ripley was able to say with complete honesty that he had expected something of the sort. "I imagine the professor will find Blue a tougher nut to crack than Samson Brant before he's through," he declared.

"Let 'em go to it," Grumpy said. "We ain't takin' sides. Whoever comes out on top will find he's holdin' a losin' hand."

Rainbow asked Yampa if he had heard anything further about Hammersley.

"Jest that he got a lot of stuff in by train from Denver an' has set up camp about three miles east of the Cross Keys house. Bought a bunch of hosses an' cowboy riggin'."

"Three miles east of the Cross Keys," Grumpy echoed suspiciously. "That puts him mighty close to Spirit Canyon. Ain't that the tip-off?"

"I'd call it a dead giveaway," Rainbow answered. "No water there, no graze for the horses. There can be only one reason for pickin that spot." He turned to Yampa. "You better go back to the Crossing."

"No need o' that," the old man told him. "Blue ain't there. Him and the rest rode away last evenin'. They're movin' down through these bluffs. I almost bumped into 'em 'bout two hours ago."

"Where's your horse?" Ripley asked.

"Back there a few yards."

"Well, you fork it and get away from us. Hole up down here somewhere and keep your eyes open. When you run out of grub come into Dan's place at night and wait around until you spot us."

About twenty minutes after they had parted company with Yampa the partners reached a rock-strewn mountain meadow. As they started across, the screeching whine of a bullet whipped over their heads. From the slope opposite came the flat, brief

124

bark of a rifle. A second shot slapped the dust out of Grumpy's hat as they darted to the cover of the first outcropping of rock. The little one grabbed his gun out of the saddle boot and returned that fire. Rainbow joined in a second later. "Aim for that big boulder just to the right of 'em—and keep your shots low! The angle is right. A slug will glance off and catch 'em where it hurts!"

There was no doubt in the mind of either but what this was Blue Morgan's bunch.

"Mebbe it's us, not Brant, that Hammersley contracted for Morgan to wipe out," Grumpy growled.

"All part of the same deal, Grump! Give it to 'em now!"

His strategy was almost immediately successful. In a few minutes Blue and his men found their position too dangerous to hold. First one and then another raced up the slope, flattened to their horses' backs. A slug from Grumpy's rifle made one of them sag limply in his saddle.

"Come on!" Rainbow commanded. "We'll get out of this jackpot while we've got the chance!"

Slipping away without drawing another shot, they swung wide of the meadow and set their course for the Priest ranch. The supper bell was ringing when they rode into the yard.

"Just in time!" Dan called to them.

The partners were surprised to see Professor Hammersley and Saburo Itchi sitting on the gallery. There was no sign of Karen, Anne, or Darwin. Grumpy's grizzled face turned grim.

"I don't savvy this," he muttered under his breath.

"Neither do I!" Rainbow's mouth had set at a hard angle. "Howie doesn't seem to be around either. We won't turn our broncs into the corral; just leave 'em at the rack."

The professor started to greet them as they stepped on the gallery, but Rainbow turned at once to Priest. "Dan, where are Miss Thane and Miss Wattress?"

"They're at the camp, Rip. They insisted that they was puttin' us out by stayin' here. When they moved Professor Darwin and Howie went along."

"It's such a short distance," Hammersley put in. "We're

back and forth several times a day. You must come over in the morning, Mr. Ripley."

"I think we'll go over tonight—right after supper," Rainbow said thinly.

"Of course. Any time," the professor agreed, his burning eyes meeting Itchi's in scarcely veiled alarm.

Suspicions and hatreds were so near the surface that conversation dried up and the evening meal was pervaded with a feeling of tenseness and conflict that even Dan caught.

"You're not eatin' like a man who's been in the saddle for a couple of days, Rip," he observed. "Let the missus git yuh somethin' else——"

"Wait!" Rainbow jerked out. "Listen a moment!"

Through the open windows came the unmistakable rattle of gunfire. Ripley and Grumpy kicked their chairs out of the way and ran to the door. The purple haze of late twilight was fading into night.

"That's comin' from the east—'bout three miles away in the direction of the camp," Grumpy cried. "You know what it means, Rainbow!"

"I'll say I do!" The tall man whirled around on Hammersley and Itchi, his face dark with wrath. "I reckon both of you know what it means too! You're well out of it, but the others aren't!"

Itchi started to his feet, indignantly protesting their innocence, but Rainbow slammed him aside.

"Dan, get up your crew and follow us!" Ripley ordered. "We're taking a hand in this business!"

Chapter Fifteen

IF IT HAD BEEN Professor Hammersley's intention to locate the camp where it would have no protection from attack he could not have selected a spot that would have served his purpose better. The first rise of low bluffs formed a half circle around it to the east. In the other direction the plateau was as flat as a board.

The flashes of gunfire in the darkening night told the partners that Blue Morgan had his men on the top of those low bluffs, from where they had the camp at their mercy.

"Get up in back of them!" Rainbow ordered. "Dan will have sense enough to swing that way!"

Samson Brant was making a fight of it. His forces had dropped back from the tents, taking their horses with them, and had spread out fanwise.

Ripley was infuriated at the thought of Karen and the others caught in the line of fire. He knew Howie would try to get them to cover, but on that flinty stretch of ground there wasn't a boulder or stringer of rock behind which even a child could seek shelter. A wagon box or a bale of hay would be the best protection they could hope to find.

Blue wasn't satisfied to remain on the bluffs when he perceived Brant's men retreating farther and farther. In an effort to drive them back into the trap he came racing down the slope at the head of his force and ran head on into Rainbow and Grumpy. The drumming of hoofs had warned the latter, and the wicked coughing of the two partners' rifles precipitately checked Morgan's wild rush. Being opposed from this unexpected direction seemed to puzzle the outlaw.

"Couple of 'em got up here" he yelled, his voice drifting down the wind to Ripley and Grumpy. "There's only two of 'em! We'll ride into the ground this time!"

Before he got his second charge organized Priest and four of his crew arrived.

"They'll come over that ridge ahead!" Rainbow told them. "When we turn 'em go after 'em! Keep 'em on the run!"

The words were barely cold on his lips when Morgan's bunch rushed. For a second he and his men were dimly outlined as they flowed over the ridge. Ahead of them half a dozen guns suddenly bloomed red in the night. Ten yards off to the right another rifle began to chatter. It was Grumpy, blocking any wild chance that the enemy might try to sweep around them.

Morgan's horse began to rear and plunge. The outlaw was here eleven strong, and men like Ruby, Crutcher, and Wild Bill were seasoned gun fighters, but though they tried to answer the blasting fire being poured into them the result of the battle was already decided. Blue recognized as much. A yell from him sent his followers scurrying back from the direction they had come.

Grumpy was after them, a shrill Injun screech of satisfaction on his lips, before Rainbow and the others could take up the chase. It was a running fight for several miles then.

"Far enough!" Rainbow cried out finally. "Hold up! You stay here a few minutes, Dan, and be ready for them if they come back! We're going down to the camp!"

"Wait a minute, Rip!" Priest called him back. "What's this all about anyway? Hammersley says it's Morgan. What's he molestin' these people for?"

"I don't know, Dan," Rainbow put him off. "There's a couple women down there. If a scratch has been put on 'em I'll have plenty to say about it. They never should have left your place!"

He was gone then, and Grumpy had to use his spurs to overtake him.

"I hate to think what we're likely to find!" the hard-bitten little man cried. "You figger Blue knew he was shootin' at wimmen?"

"No," said Rainbow decisively. "Hammersley fixed that up! Give Brant a yell! We don't want to run into a shot from them!"

Brant had followed the fight on the bluffs with astonished eyes. He knew help had come from somewhere and that Morgan's gang had been driven off.

"It must be Hammersley and the Cross Keys punchers!" he called out to his men. Two of them were down, seriously

128

wounded. One lay dead. "We'll move this blasted camp to-morrow or know the reason why!"

Grumpy's call reached them a few minutes later.

"That's Gibbs!" Ginger Revell cried. "It's him and Ripley! They saved our skins this time!"

Grumpy called again, and Brant answered: "Over here!"

The partners swung their broncs that way at a driving gallop and pulled up so sharply they set the animals back on their haunches.

"Much obliged to you!" Brant hailed them. "You didn't owe us any favors after that misunderstanding in Brown's Park——"

"Where's Miss Thane?" Rainbow cut in brusquely.

"The last I saw of her she was with Darwin and Hallett. They had both women with them and were running toward the bluffs. Did you leave Hammersley and Itchi on the slope?"

"We left them back at the Cross Keys house— where they weren't in any danger of having a slug find them! Think that over, Brant! Maybe somebody's taking you for a sucker!"

Pulling his horse to a gallop, Rainbow rode through the camp and beyond, with Grumpy sticking close to him.

"Rip, is that you?" a cry reached them.

"Howie!" Rainbow answered tensely. They swung toward him. "You're alone! What does it mean?"

"Ease up," Hallett told him. "We're all right. I got Miss Thane and Miss Wattress in under the bluffs. It was the only place I could find——"

"You couldn't have done better." Rainbow didn't attempt to dissemble his relief. With the next breath, however, he let Howie feel his indignation. "Why did you and Darwin ever let them leave Dan's place? I warned you to keep them there!"

"We tried, Rip! When we told 'em they'd be safer there they wanted to know safer from what. What could we do? We couldn't say a word without tellin' 'em everythin'!"

"I'm sorry," muttered Rainbow. "Your hands were tied. They're going back to the ranch tonight if I have my way."

Three evenly spaced shots sounded up on the slope.

"Who's that?" Hallett demanded.

"Dan and his crew," Grumpy informed him. "I'll answer his signal. I reckon he wants to come down."

As they walked to the base of the bluffs Rainbow acquainted Howie with Hammersley's latest move.

"That's purty, ain't it?" Hallett muttered savagely. "How much longer you goin' to hold off, Rip?"

"We've got to hold off until we get a line on where the silk is cached. But I just dropped a bug in Brant's ear that may help things along."

"Don't try that with the girl," Hallett warned. "Jim made a couple of hints and she shut him up promptly. She shore won't take it from you. She waits on that uncle of hers and worries about him like he was a child."

The dead blackness of early evening was turning to silver as the moon swung higher. Rainbow could see Karen and the others watching them.

"Rainbow! Grumpy!" Karen called and ran to them. "What an experience! It was Morgan, I suppose?"

"No supposing about it," Ripley replied grimly. "It was!"

Anne and Darwin joined them.

"Grumpy, I don't think I was ever so glad to see anyone as you and your partner!" Miss Wattress sighed heavily.

"Waal, we're always turnin' up," the little man grinned. "Like a couple o' bad pennies."

"I notice you never turn up but what you're needed. I couldn't go through this again. I'm going back to Mrs. Priest tonight."

"So are you, Karen," Rainbow said tightly. "This raid is most likely to be repeated."

"Why should they bother us?" she demanded, her voice unsteady and puzzled. "What have we got that they want?"

Ripley felt Darwin's silent warning to say nothing. "You will have to ask Professor Hammersley," was his sober answer. "I think all of us are entitled to an explanation."

"I am sure the doctor will be quite willing to give you

130

one." It was the velvety, well-mannered voice of Saburo Itchi. Unnoticed, he had come up in back of them. "We secured a wagon and drove out as quickly as possible," he continued. "The doctor is looking after some of Mr. Brant's men; two of them are in serious condition. I dread to think what might have happened but for your prompt action, Mr. Ripley."

Back at the camp a fire had been lighted.

"That's purty foolish," growled Grumpy. "It's askin' for a shot!"

"The doctor is convinced we will not be attacked again to-night," the Japanese told him.

"He'd know, I reckon," the little man said with sharp insinuation.

At the camp they learned that Hammersley was in the tent in which the wounded had been placed. In addition to the two men he was attending several others who had received superficial wounds. Priest and his punchers had arrived. They had not yet got down from their saddles.

"We had a look around up there, Rip," Dan said. "Blue must have carried off two or three of his gang that won't do any more ridin'. There's blood all over the rocks. Yuh want us to stick around a mite longer?"

"Yes, Dan. We'll be going back to the house with you. Miss Thane and Miss Wattress are going too."

"Rainbow, I can't leave Uncle," Karen protested. "My place is here with him; the rest of you go. You don't notice it, I know, but Uncle is near the breaking point. Everything has gone so badly for him."

"We'll put it up to him when he comes out," Ripley said flatly.

Itchi had stepped inside with Hammersley. Ten minutes or more passed before they emerged together. The professor went to Karen at once and expressed his relief at finding her un-harmed.

"I understand that Mr. Ripley feels you would be safer at

the house, my dear," he told her. "If it will not be imposing on Mrs. Priest I think you should go."

It was unexpected, but Rainbow saw in it a move to put off being questioned. He did not intend to let it go at that, but it was not necessary for him to say anything as Karen demanded the explanation Itchi had promised the professor would give them.

"I think this can be all traced back to that incident in Black Forks," Hammersley said. "We have had several samples of Morgan's attempts to get revenge. This appears to be his latest effort. . . . I'll walk over to the wagon with you, Karen. You can have your things brought in in the morning."

Brant, standing a few feet away, had heard all this.

"You ain't thinking of quitting the camp yourself, are you, Hammersley?" The tone of the question was sharper than he had ever used to the professor. Rainbow and Grumpy correctly surmised the reason.

"That bug he had dropped in his ear is beginnin' to itch," the little one told himself.

"Certainly not, Brant," Hammersley answered. "These wounded men need my attention."

At the wagon he had more to say. His voice dropped cautiously as he addressed himself to Ripley. "What I said was for Brant's ears. I have tried to keep this from you," he said. "The truth is that Brant and his men are all desperate characters, fully as dangerous as Morgan. I have known it for some time. There is a deeper grudge between the two than the shooting of Chink Johnson."

"You knew these men were outlaws and still kept them in your employ, Uncle?" Karen asked incredulously.

"I ask you to understand my position," he replied. "I can't afford to break with them. They do their work well, and they know how to handle a boat. I could not get anyone to take their place. If I dismissed them it would mean the expedition could not go on. But I can't say any more now; Brant is looking this way."

Rainbow and Grumpy sat out on the gallery of the Cross

Keys house late that night, speaking in hushed voices.

"That confidential story of Hammersley's proves one thing," the tall man murmured. "He doesn't know how fully we understand every move he's made. He really thought he was fooling us."

A low whistle reached them as they sat there. It was repeated a moment later.

"That meant for us?" Grumpy questioned. "Came from over there by the barn."

"Let's walk over that way," Rainbow suggested. He gave his gun belt a hitch as he walked across the yard. Grumpy was ready for a surprise too.

"It's me, Yampa!" came a low cry as they turned the corner of the building.

"I didn't expect to find you here so soon," declared Rainbow. "What is it?"

"Rip, I found a body floatin' in the river when I went down for water about sunset. Caught on some rocks, it was. I hauled it out. Little bald-headed feller. I went through his pockets and read some of his papers. His name was Potts. Appears he was with the perfessor's crowd. Been in the water four-five days."

"Dr. Potts, eh?" Rainbow looked at Grumpy. "I knew they had drowned him."

"Drowned nuthin'!" Yampa muttered testily. "This feller was shot! Got a bullet hole square between the eyes!"

"Waal, that *is* news" said Grumpy. "Killed him, the dirty skunks! But who did it, Rainbow?"

"I don't know. Maybe Itchi—or Hammersley, or any one one of them. I know what you're thinking, but I am afraid we'll never be able to pin this murder on the man who did the job. . . . Where did you leave the body, Yampa?"

"I brought it in. Got it over there on my saddle."

"Fine! We'll put it in the barn until morning."

"What's the idea o' that?" Grumpy demanded, his eyes deeply puzzled. "If it won't do us any good the least we should think of is sendin' it into Vernal to an undertaker.

Yampa can just say he found it and doesn't know anythin'. You said yourself we can't prove who killed Dr. Potts."

"I know"—Ripley nodded—"but maybe Samson Brant will tell us."

Chapter Sixteen

A WORD to Dan, first thing in the morning, about what was inside the barn resulted in a lock being put on the doors.

"I don't want anything said about this," Rainbow told the rancher. "As soon as we've had breakfast Grumpy and I will ride out to the camp. I'm going to try to bring Brant back with us. We can build a box then and give the body temporary burial."

Karen and Anne joined them at the table.

"You girls look a mite peaked this mornin'," Mrs. Priest declared. "An' why not, after the goin's on last night? Laws, I don't know what this country is comin' to! Thought rustlers was bad enough!"

"If they don't eat hearty it ain't no reflection on yore cookin', Miz Priest," Grumpy told her. "Them sour-cream pancakes just seem to slip down like they was glad to git acquainted with you!"

"Last night seems like a bad dream," Karen said. "I lay awake for hours. . . . There wasn't any more shooting, Rainbow?"

"No, everything was quiet. Grumpy and I are going out to the camp directly. Howie can drive out and bring your things in."

Ripley saw her pale cheeks go whiter suddenly. "Something has happened!" she exclaimed, rising. "Here come Uncle and Mr. Itchi! They're walking in!"

Rainbow saw that the manner of the two men was excited. In the Japanese it was unusual enough to make Ripley wonder if it was not being put on for a purpose.

"Well, it's happened!" the professor exclaimed as he stepped through the door. "Brant and I have reached the parting of the ways!"

Grumpy flicked a quick glance at Rainbow. "That came pretty sudden, didn't it?" the latter queried. "What happened?"

"He insisted that we move at once," replied the professor. "I was quite willing to agree to that, but I did not propose to do it in the middle of the night. I did not intend to have my authority questioned either. The man was insufferable! I told them to take the horses and their personal effects and clear out. There is nothing for me to do now but send for a new crew—men who have had river experience. And we must have a cook at once. I was hoping we could get a team from you, Mr. Priest."

"Shore," Dan said. "We need a few things in Vernal. You can fetch them for us."

"What about Jim?" demanded Karen anxiously. "Have you left him in camp alone?"

"He's perfectly safe, my dear. As soon as we return from town I shall have everything moved to a more protected location."

Karen was not satisfied. She turned to Rainbow. "I don't like the idea of Jim's being there alone. He hasn't only Morgan, but Brant, to fear now. There's no telling what those desperadoes will do."

"I believe you're needlessly worrying yourself this time," Ripley assured her. "Those two aren't interested in Jim Darwin."

The partners waited until Hammersley and Itchi had departed for town before they themselves pulled away from the ranch.

"The old coot tried to put a smooth face on this break with

Brant," Grumpy grumbled contemptuously. "It didn't take that gent long to figger out that he had got the double double-cross. I bet they was callin' each other by their right names and then some!"

"Yes," Rainbow muttered with a frosty smile. "But it's another trick for us. Brant will be looking for a chance to turn on Hammersley. We'll give him one before the day's over."

They found Darwin at the camp. "They had a terrible row," the young scientist told them. "I was in my tent when it started. I tried to catch what it was about, but big Gass stopped me when I stepped out and told me to go back to bed. I wasn't in any position to argue with him. I could hear that fellow with the long chin—Ginger Revell—threatening to kill both Hammersley and Itchi. I actually believe if I hadn't been here the two of them would have been killed."

"The professor says he give 'em some horses an'——" Grumpy started to say.

"Gave them?" Jim exclaimed sarcastically. "They took what they wanted and made him like it!"

"Where's Brant now?" asked Rainbow.

"Up on the rim somewhere. You know what they're after. . . . I suppose Karen is worried about my being here alone."

"Yes. But you're safe enough. I told her so. Howie will be out directly. We'll try to find Brant. I've got a little surprise for him."

He told Darwin what he meant, and also thought it best to acquaint him with the sell-out Hammersley had given Brant.

"I guess you know where that leaves you," Jim said, visibly alarmed. "Hammersley has put a price on your heads. You'll be picked off the first chance that offers!"

"Well, we've had the blackball put on us before and lived through it." Grumpy's voice had a grim ring.

"When will I be seeing you again?" Darwin called as they rode off.

"Most any time!" Rainbow told him. "We won't be far away!"

With a cautiousness that had become habitual with them they reached the rim. In the course of half an hour they caught a distant glimpse of riders. They were able to cut the distance in half without being observed.

"It's Brant," declared Grumpy. "They're scourin' the rim as hard as we did."

A few minutes later Rainbow said: "Give 'em a yell. I'll wave my hat at 'em."

The men swung their horses around and reached for their guns. They stood in that position, dangerously alert until they recognized the partners.

"You up here keeping cases on us?" Brant demanded with cool hostility. "You did us a favor last night, but don't let it go to your head. I'm done with Hammersley, and I am dead willing to be done with you. I've got a couple of badly wounded men with me. I'm going to find a spot to camp along this rim and stay here until they're fit to travel. Does that answer what's on your mind?"

"No," Rainbow replied. "I want you to ride into the ranch for a few minutes. It won't take you long. I've got something to show you that may interest you. You can come alone or bring your men. . . . I didn't tell you wrong last night, did I?"

Brant thought it over for a minute.

. "You're pretty deep, Ripley, but if you give me your word that this isn't a trick I'll go with you."

"You've got my word for it," Rainbow said without hesitation.

It took them less than an hour and a half to reach the house. The yard was deserted at this time of the day. As they rode in Dan stepped out of the kitchen.

"The women around?" Ripley asked.

"Miss Thane is restin', an' Miss Wattress is down under the cottonwoods beyond the corral doin' some sketchin'. Yuh want me to call 'em?"

"No, just unlock the barn for us. I want to show Brant what we've got."

Samson Brant hung back suspiciously as the door was opened.

"Go ahead," Rainbow told him. "It's all right." He pulled back the canvas tarp that covered the body of Dr. Potts. "Brant—who killed him?" was his sharp question.

Brant's eyes narrowed to slits in his hard face. "I don't know," he growled, overcoming the shock of his surprise. "I had nothing to do with it."

"I'm not accusing you," said Rainbow. "But it's murder. The gun was held right up to his face. Whoever gets this job pinned on him won't be around to get in anyone's way."

Brant understood him and was tempted. Behind his vacant, staring eyes his thoughts were racing. With an effort he pulled himself out of his trancelike state, and his decision was made. "No," he said heavily, "I don't know anything about it!"

"All right, if that's the way you want it," said Ripley. "It will keep, should you change your mind. I'm sorry I bothered you."

Brant rode away, hunched over in deep abstraction.

"He's already wonderin' if he made a mistake," Grumpy muttered.

"Let it go; it was worth trying." Rainbow's tone was brusque with disappointment. "Dan, can we knock a box together in a hurry and put the body in the ground without having to answer any questions?"

"Yeah. There's lumber up there on the rafters and plenty of tools here. I'll hitch a team and back the wagon into the barn. We can bury him over in the draw."

Driving back to the ranch at noon, their grisly task finished, Ripley said: "That's a heathen way to put a fine little man under the ground. I'll make it my business to see that he isn't there long."

The crew had come in from the north range for dinner. On the Cross Keys the help were served first. Mrs. Priest and the Mexican woman who did most of the cooking, were ready for them. The men ate with a great seriousness and, save for a muttered "Pass the butter" or "Pass the potatoes," had nothing to say. When they were finished they filed out of the house and seemed to find their usual loquaciousness the moment they were out of earshot of Karen and Anne on the gallery. Karen noticed and spoke to Mrs. Priest about it.

"I'm afraid our being here is responsible," she said ruefully.

"Laws, no!" Mrs. Priest laughed. "A body can never git a word out of 'em around the house, but they'll chatter like a flock of magpies once they git by themselves."

After dinner Anne started back to the spot where she had been sketching, and at her invitation Rainbow accompanied her. "I wanted to talk to you," she explained. "I've definitely decided not to go on with the expedition, and I don't think Karen should be permitted to do so either. Jim Darwin agrees with me, but he is so madly in love with her that he doesn't know how to be stern and uncompromising. I think Karen would take it from you, though, Rainbow. She has a tremendous respect for you."

"I don't believe Professor Hammersley will get things reorganized in time to go on this year," Rainbow said, thinking that respect without affection was a cold, lifeless thing that held no promise of happiness. "But I agree with you that Karen shouldn't go on. I suppose the summer can be counted as lost for you."

"No, this country with its splendid color entrances me. I can't accomplish much now with what materials I have, but I've sent for some things that should be here soon."

Rainbow ran through her sketches as she went to work.

"What are these?" he asked, holding up some drawings. "Indian pueblos?"

"No, those are cliff dwellings—some things I've been trying to work up for Jim from his description of the ruins he discovered last fall down in southwestern Colorado on the Rio Mancos."

"Well, they're interesting," Rainbow volunteered. "What is this circular thing in the center? A watchtower or some means of getting out to the rim of the canyon?"

Anne shook her head. "I don't know too much about it. Jim says they were sun worshippers and that in every dwelling—maybe of twenty to thirty compartments—he has always found this circular room. He thinks it was used for religious rites of some sort. An *estufa*, he calls it. He could tell you all about it if you're interested."

Ripley was more interested than he cared to admit.

"They'd be big enough to store a lot of stuff in," he observed. "Darwin never said anything like this had been found around here, did he?"

"I can't recall that he did." Anne smiled. "Why this sudden interest in cliff dwellings, Rainbow?"

"Oh, it just fits in with something I've been thinking about for some time. I'll have to speak to Jim."

He proceeded to do so at once and for the second time that day he and Grumpy rode out to the camp.

"There's no record of the cliff dwellers having lived this far up the river," Darwin told them. "But so little is known about them that it would be foolish to say they weren't here. Certainly they were on the Colorado. Some fine examples down in the Canyon de Chelly." He thought he knew what was in Rainbow's mind. "You think they may have found some ruins and stored the silk there?"

"Naturally. Grump, tell Darwin what you were saying to me about that garden on the rim. What Dr. Potts told you."

Before the little man was half finished Jim began to exhibit signs of excitement. "You're absolutely right!" he burst out. "If you found soil up there where it doesn't naturally belong you've stumbled upon a prehistoric garden! The fact that there's water makes me doubly sure!"

"Hammersley and Itchi would recognize it as well as you, wouldn't they?" asked Ripley. "They were out here before."

"Of course they would! I tell you you've hit it!" Jim glanced at his watch. "It's not three o'clock yet. Hammersley can't possibly be back before dark. Suppose we go up on the rim

140

and confirm all this. I've felt rather useless around here, but maybe I can be of some service, after all."

"Before you go flyin' off half-cocked just remember what you told us this mornin'," Grumpy put in soberly. "There's plenty of guns on that rim with itchin' triggers. I don't say we can't go up there and back without gettin' a slug between the shoulders, but that's the chance we're takin'."

"If you're willing to take that chance so am I," Darwin answered.

"Get your horse then," said Rainbow.

Leading the ascent, he struck up through the bluffs and made no attempt to reach the rim until they had worked far enough north to be able to cut over to it at a point close to their proposed destination. He had every reason to believe that Morgan and his men had not quit these bluffs. If the outlaws were not moving through them, they were holed up somewhere, licking their wounds and getting ready for another foray. Brant and his forces could be regarded as equally dangerous now.

In the red dust at the bottom of a narrow defile between the split halves of a small sandstone butte Grumpy read a story. "Number of horses passed here purty recent," he declared. "They was goin' the same direction we are."

"How recent would you say?" Rainbow asked with tight-lipped concern.

"Two-three hours. Not more."

"Let's turn back a few yards and crawl up on top that ragged peak," the tall man said. "It's high enough to give us a look around. We can't be half a mile from where we're going."

Reaching the peak, they left their horses and made their way on hand and foot to the crest. The rim stretched away in either direction for miles. Ahead of them lay the garden. At sight of it a low whistle of surprise escaped Grumpy.

"Well, I'm askin' you if that ain't a tough break?" he grunted fiercely. "That's Brant's bunch—camped right where we bedded down the other night!"

"It's Brant, all right," Rainbow confirmed. "They didn't pick that spot just because they found water there. They had some idea of where they cached the silk, even though it was done at night. When they saw that creek tumbling down the gorge they knew they had found the place." He turned to Darwin. "This stops us! If we try to go down there it will be a case of shooting it out with them. The first shot will bring Blue into the ruckus and we'll be caught on two sides. . . . You can't tell anything from here, can you, Jim?"

"I certainly can!" Darwin said emphatically. "There's nothing but rock in every direction except right there in the cup around the springs. That soil was carried there on the backs of men and women. You looked down over the edge of the rim and saw nothing. You wouldn't; the wall evidently cuts back in, and on that recess you'll find cliff dwellings!"

"You can't be wrong," Rainbow declared with complete conviction. "There're some of those old stone houses here, and when we get into them we'll find the silk!"

Chapter Seventeen

*U*NAWARE that they were being watched, Brant and his men moved around on the rim, studying the ground and the rocky surface just beyond. They were obviously searching for some hidden, secret way of getting down to the ruins.

Stretched out on the peak, Darwin observed them with absorbed interest.

"You're pretty sure there is a passageway leading below?" Rainbow asked.

"Absolutely! The cliff dwellers always selected inaccessible places for their buildings, but they had to have an easy and practical way of getting their food in."

142

"Would it lead up from that little circular room that seemed to be set right in the center of the houses in the drawings?"

"No, the *estufas* were only for religious purposes, Rainbow. The secret entrance may have reached the surface any place within an area several hundred yards square. But I'd start looking for it in the garden. That's where they're usually found. I suppose they placed them there because it was the easiest way of protecting the entrance. In case of attack, they would leave a man on the surface to cover the passage with earth and sacrifice himself for the good of the clan."

"Huntin' for it sounds like a long job to me," commented Grumpy. "Might take us ten days, even if there was no one to bother us."

"I daresay it took Hammersley and Itchi that long," Jim agreed. "There's another way, of course. We could put a rope ladder over the rim and I could climb down to the bench. I've always built my own ladders, so I know how to do it. We'd need three or four hundred feet of good Mexican hemp line. I suppose we could get it in Vernal——"

"How long would it take you to put it together?" Ripley queried.

"Two or three days—sticking to it."

Rainbow shook his head. "We can't wait that long, Jim! Brant is where he wants to be, and he'll put up a fight to stay there. But I figure he'll be run off. If that happens, and the coast is clear for an hour or two, we've got to be ready to take advantage of it. We can get all the rope we need from Priest. A piece of good *maguey* ought to be strong enough for us; that kind of rope can hold a steer. We can make a harness out of one end of it, and I'll let the two of you lower me over."

"I've done crazy things like that," Darwin said with a grave smile. "When we're ready I'll be the one to go over. I know more about these things than you do, Rainbow; I can find the entrance from below and open it."

"Can one man do it?" Grumpy demanded skeptically.

143

"That slab of stone must weigh a heap. An' how do you know it'll work?"

"It must have worked for Hammersley," Jim answered. "As for the weight, that's nothing. Those ancient men were excellent masons. You'll find that stone cut so that the weight is all in the heel of it. If there wasn't a foot or more of earth on top of it you could raise it with one hand."

A warning whistle reached them, and they looked below to see old Yampa gesticulating at them excitedly. "Get down from there, yuh idyits!" the old man yelled. "Do yuh wannta git yore heads blowed off? There's a scrap comin' here in a few minutes that'll curl yore hair! It won't take either side three jerks of a bull's tail to figger that whoever gets hold of this yere peak is boss! Look over to the north 'bout six hundred yards—jest below that rockfall!"

"By thunder, it's Morgan!" Grumpy burst out. "Here they come!"

Counting himself, Blue had nine men still able to ride. That it was their intention to reach the peak and from there blast Brant off the rim was immediately apparent. But they had barely broken cover when Ginger Revell snapped a quick shot at them. In two or three seconds every gun was bucking.

"Come on!" Rainbow ordered. "If this goes our way we'll be back here tonight!"

Yampa led them down the defile and over a crumbling dike. Half a mile more and they were able to look back in time to see Blue's forces reach the peak. Brant was fighting back stubbornly, but he had lost the decision already, as Yampa had predicted. Morgan was now able to rake the rim with the fire of his guns. In ten minutes or less there wasn't a man left on the rimrock around the garden. With Brant's force demoralized and fleeing, Morgan left the peak and chased after them.

"I guess that means tonight or never for us," said Ripley. "Yampa, do you know the place they call the Pot Holes?"

"Yep."

"You wait there for us. We'll be back tonight. We'll leave the horses with you then and get back in here on foot."

Yampa eyed him with an obscure interest but said nothing.

Parting company with the old man a few minutes later, the partners and Darwin rode back to the ranch. The sun was down by the time they reached the deserted camp.

"You better leave your stuff there and tell Hammersley tomorrow that you're through," Rainbow advised Darwin. "Karen will just think you rode in with us for supper. Don't tell her any different. About midnight we can start back for the rim. If we find things still favorable we'll try to get over the wall as soon as the sky begins to brighten."

After supper they sat out on the gallery with Karen, Anne, and the Priests for an hour. It was a mild evening, and Dan's pipe had a pleasant aroma. Grumpy and Dan did most of the talking. They secretly liked to be drawn out about their younger days, and Anne had no difficulty in keeping the conversation lively. Rainbow's glance went to Darwin and Karen, seated together in the deep shadows in the corner. They were quiet, apparently content just to be together. The thought struck a chord of loneliness in him.

"Foolish to feel that way about it," he mused. "Things are getting pretty bad when a rolling stone begins to feel sorry for himself."

The professor and Itchi drove into the yard about nine. Grumpy's eyes narrowed as he caught sight of the mousy little man in the rear of the wagon. He found a chance to express himself to Rainbow as the others went out to speak to Hammersley. "If that's the new cook Blue must have supplied him," he muttered. "That's Smoky Yeager!"

"So I noticed." Ripley walked over to the wagon and gave Dan a hand with the things that were to be carried into the house. In the kitchen he said: "Dan, you've got several hundred feet of rope in the barn. I'm going to borrow it tonight. If I injure it at all I'll have the company make good."

"That part of it's all right," the rancher told him. "But what are yuh up to?"

"We think we've found the silk. Suppose you go out and tell Hammersley to use the team to get back to camp, and don't let the missus offer to get them anything to eat. I want to get rid of them."

Priest scratched his head dubiously. "Waal, I'll try. But yuh know Emmy!"

He got out in time to take his wife aside before she asked the two men in. A few minutes later Rainbow heard the wagon moving away. Karen and Anne retired soon after.

"What did you tell Hammersley?" Ripley asked Jim.

"I said I'd be out later. I don't think he suspected anything, but Itchi gave me a look. There's a queer mental relationship between those two men, Rainbow. I felt it long before I came West with them this spring. Have you noticed that they never disagree? One mind is a perfect echo of the other."

"I'll say I've noticed it," Ripley acknowledged. "Hammersley is arrogant and domineering, but it's the Jap, for all his groveling and bootlicking, who's the boss. I've wondered sometimes if he doesn't have the professor hypnotized."

"It is a hypnosis of a sort," Darwin told him. "That's the only way a man can dominate another person's mind. It doesn't make Hammersley any less guilty; he was whipped into line by definite criminal impulses of his own.

Priest walked across the yard from the barn. "I've set the rope out for you, Rip. Howie goin' with yuh?"

"Yes."

"If yuh need another man——" Dan offered.

"No. But there *is* something you can do. If we're not back by noon tomorrow get word to Asa Sharp at Mormon Valley. Tell him to look for us up on the rim."

They left about twenty minutes later, passing to the north of the camp. Not a light burned.

"Do you think there's any chance that Morgan's bunch may be down there?" Darwin asked.

146

"It'll be bad for our plans if they are," said Rainbow. "He had Brant on the run this afternoon, but that wasn't the end of it. They're maybe twelve-fifteen miles from here now and still shooting it out. In this broken country there are a lot of places where you can fort up and get your second wind. Brant will take advantage of them. If he's cornered he'll try to slip away during the night. Morgan will stick close to him. That's the only way we figure to have a chance."

They found Yampa waiting at the Pot Holes. He was able to confirm Rainbow's surmise to some extent.

"There was gunfire to the south off an' on till dark," he told them. "I drifted down the rim a few miles. I saw Tay Crutcher all folded up on some rocks, deader'n a smoked herrin'. That's a little more interest on the account I got agin' that bunch! Yuh foller me now an' I'll show yuh where to put the hosses so no one will be runnin' into 'em."

In single file they squeezed in between boulders the size of a house and found themselves in a natural rock-walled corral.

"Satisfy yuh?" queried Yampa.

"Fine!" Rainbow told him. "Been close to this place a number of times and never knew it was here. . . . Will you be around when we get back?"

"I'll be around somewheres," was the old man's vague answer.

Without their knowing it, he followed them until they were just below the rim. He dropped back then and reconnoitered through the bluffs for the rest of the night. He had asked no questions about the purpose of this night trip to the rim, but he had observed the heavy coil of rope that Rainbow and Howie had carried between them, and it had told him enough.

Dawn was still some minutes away when Rainbow reached the old garden and signaled the others that they had the place to themselves. Darwin had already prepared the loops in the rope. He superintended laying it out so it could be paid off without any chance of knotting.

"I'm more excited about this than you are, Rainbow," he

147

said tensely. "I've got a double stake. We're both interested in finding the silk, but if I can get a cliff dwelling along with it, it will be a real thrill."

He crawled out to the very lip of the rim and located a spot where the wall was smooth.

"I'll go over right here," he told them. "The three of you stay back thirty to forty feet and pay the line out slowly so it won't burn on the rocks. If I want to be hauled up I'll slap the line sharply three times. You'll feel the vibrations. If the shelf is there you'll know when I've reached it by the slack."

"I guess we've got all that," declared Rainbow. "No matter what happens we won't leave you hung up here. If we get into trouble we'll haul you out before we fire a shot."

Lying down on the rim, Darwin inched away until he had a tight line behind him. Slowly then he slipped over the edge.

Ripley tried to estimate how much rope they were paying out. "That must be fifty feet now," he said.

The pull of Darwin's weight continued steady for another estimated twenty feet. Suddenly the rope went slack.

"By grab, he's made it!" Grumpy got out tightly. Ripley and Hallett joined in his sigh of relief.

"I suppose it will be some time before we get any sign of where Jim's trying to open the passage," Rainbow told them. "We'll leave the rope where it is, in case we have to pull him up. Meanwhile we might spread out a little and watch for some movement in the earth."

Mists were rising from the river. To the east the sun was giving a magnificent warning of its coming. Rainbow's glance ran over the rim and to the peak from which they had witnessed the beginning of the fight. "If we can only have about an hour here we'll be all right," he thought.

He kept moving around, eyes on the ground. The minutes had begun to drag. Every one that ticked away lessened their chances, and Rainbow was keenly aware of it.

"Rip! Grump!" It was a sharp, low cry from Howie. "Look here!"

The two men ran to where he was pointing at a trembling crack in the earth.

"That's it" Grumpy whipped out. "Scoop the earth out with yore hands! Hurry up!"

The outline of the slab of stone became definite, the dry soil filtering through the cracks.

"You there, Jim?" Ripley called.

"Yeah!" came the muffled answer. "Get back! I think I've got it this time!"

With fascinated eyes they watched the stone slowly lift. Darwin's grinning face appeared in the opening.

"No need to tell you!" He beamed at them. "It's here!"

"The silk?" Grumpy demanded, his throat dry with excitement.

"Yeah! Come on down and have a look at it!"

The worn stone stairs were dark until the light streaming in from below struck them. The sight that met the men's eyes at the bottom silenced them for a minute.

"You wouldn't believe all this was here," Ripley said, deeply impressed. "Room after room! This bench must be twenty-five feet deep and I wouldn't guess how long!"

"The weather has been at work," Jim told them. "Snow drifts in and freezes. You follow me now and I'll show you what we came to see."

Climbing through the openings that led from one apartment to the next, they reached the room where Hammersley had had the bales stored.

"By Christopher, there it is!" Grumpy cried. "High and dry and safe to stay here a year or two!"

Rainbow looked down the rock wall to the river, trying to discover how the silk had been carried up. Darwin showed him where the path started over the wall.

"I reckon we've seen enough," Grumpy warned. "We've got the place marked and know how to get to it now. If we're smart we'll clear out."

"You're right," Rainbow agreed. "We want to be moving."

Darwin led the way to the foot of the stairs and started up.

149

He had taken about fifteen steps when a startled cry broke from him.

"What is it Jim?" Ripley jerked out.

"The entrance! It's closed!"

"It must have fallen——"

"Not on your life! Somebody's shut it on us!"

They reached the stone slab quickly and put their shoulders to it, but it refused to budge. With set, grim faces they looked at one another.

"If there's any doubt about what it means let's look for the rope," Jim said. "If that's gone we've got the answer!"

They returned to the bench only to find no sign of the rope. Taking off his hat, Rainbow held it out where the line had dangled. Instantly a shot rang out.

"Morgan——" muttered Howie.

"No, that shot was fired from a short-barreled automatic," Rainbow declared. "We can charge this up to Itchi. He's got us this time!"

"During the night we can go down the wall to the river," Darwin suggested.

Rainbow shook his head. "That's as far as we'd get without boats. It's no use, Jim! We're sealed up here like bugs in a bottle!"

Chapter Eighteen

SHORTLY AFTER RETURNING with the new cook Saburo Itchi had stolen away from camp to roam the bluffs and rim in quest of information concerning Brant and Blue Morgan. Horses were not for him. On foot, a shadowy, grimly malign figure, he covered untold miles. His discovery of the body of Tay Crutcher gave him his first inkling of the fight that had gone so disastrously for Samson Brant. Tireless, un-feeling, he had gone on and reached the vicinity of the garden above the cliff dwellings in time to see Rainbow and the others descending into the secret passage.

"Only Darwin could have discovered it for them," he told himself. "He shall die here with them for his trouble."

Closing the trap on the four men and rolling boulders over it to insure against its being opened took Itchi only a few minutes, his exultation lending him a double strength. He re-placed the earth then and smoothed it over. Disposing of the rope was accomplished simply by carrying it to the edge of the rim and letting it slide down the wall into the river. He was staring after it when he saw a hat below and fired a shot at it.

Knowing he had missed did not disturb him; the pigeons were safely locked up in their cage.

"It marks the end of two very colorful careers," Itchi mused, with a tight little half-smile. "Mr. Ripley and his partner should have confined themselves to chasing rustlers."

Satisfied with his success, he left the rim and began to pick his way back to camp. If he was a shadowy figure as he slipped down through the bluffs, there was soon another, equally ghostly, following him, and that dirty, tobacco-stained watcher of these dim trails amused himself by lining up the sights of his rifle on the Japanese.

"That Jap ain't been up to no good," Yampa told himself. "If I didn't figger it would be playin' right into Blue's hand I'd split the little yaller punkin' wide open and watch the seeds fly!"

The old man trailed Itchi all the way down to the low bluffs above camp. His eyes popped as he caught a distant glimpse of the new cook.

"So that's the way things go!" he snorted. "I'm a six-legged gopher if that little varmint is here jest to do the cookin'!"

On the instant Yampa decided to lay out and watch the camp for a few hours.

Down below, the professor stepped out of his tent to greet

151

Itchi. The latter's news was of such a startling nature that Hammersley forgot the mousy little man at the fire who pretended to be busy with his pots but had his ears open.

"Marvelous!" the professor cried, rubbing his hands in his glee. "Marvelous, my friend! This is better than anything we could have planned! They have found the silk, and now let them eat it!"

"The cook, Doctor," Itchi reminded him.

Hammersley lowered his voice, but Smoky caught the words "garden . . . Darwin . . . rope." He put Itchi's breakfast on the table and hovered near until he was bluntly told to withdraw.

"I'm afraid our cook has very large ears, Doctor."

"We shall have to be careful," Hammersley agreed. "We are now rid of our two most dangerous enemies!" He drew down the corners of his mouth in a forbidding manner. "I only wish the girl was in there with them!"

"Doesn't it come to the same thing, Doctor?" Itchi murmured softly. "We have Professor Darwin."

"You're right! I hadn't thought of that. But did you see anything of Brant or Morgan?"

"There has been a clash between them. Violent, I believe." The Nipponese explained about finding Crutcher. "I predict we shall be hearing from Mr. Morgan before the day is out."

Horsemen appeared on the bluffs shortly before noon. After a careful inspection of the camp one of them rode in. Itchi put a pair of glasses on the rider.

"This is Mr. Morgan now," he announced.

Blue got a minor surprise of his own when he saw Smoky there. "Nice work," he said under his breath as he passed the fire. "They don't know we're acquainted?"

"No," grunted Smoky.

"Well, Morgan," Hammersley greeted their visitor, "I hope you have news for us."

"I got news all right," Blue informed them. "You can count Brant out of this fight. He's got a few men left with him, but they don't want no more of this; they know they're licked. They'll be driftin' out of the country first chance they get."

Hammersley's cup of satisfaction overflowed on hearing this. Even Itchi showed his teeth appreciatively.

"Don't get the idea we wasn't in a fight," Blue said grimly. "I lost another man, and a couple of the boys need a doctor. Can you patch 'em up, Hammersley?"

"I'll try," the professor replied. "I'm not a surgeon, but I have some skill. Where are the men?"

"They're waitin' up there. I'll wave 'em in." The men on the bluff answered his signal and started down the slope. Blue turned back to the professor and Itchi with a dour look. "What about Ripley and Gibbs? Have you seen any more of 'em?"

"Mr. Morgan, those gentlemen have been removed," the Japanese said quietly. "You can forget about them."

Blue's lip curled away from his teeth forbiddingly. "Come on, let's have the rest of it," he demanded with a dangerous thinness. "There better be no secrets between us!"

Itchi's eyes were inscrutable in his wooden face. He had caught the threat in Morgan's demand. "The two men can be considered dead," he said. "You would do well not to inquire into the details."

"All right," Blue muttered. He was just waiting, not agreeing to anything. He intended to take over as soon as he discovered where the silk was cached. If Smoky failed to get that information for him he would force it out of Hammersley.

The arrival of Ben Ruby and the others gave Morgan a chance to exchange a word with the cook.

"How did you get this job?" he asked Yeager.

"They showed up in Vernal. When I heard they was lookin' fer a cook I went after 'em, Blue. I figgered yuh'd want me to."

Morgan nodded. "What have you heard?"

"The Jap's got Ripley and Gibbs and a couple others trapped somewheres. The old man was awful excited about it."

"Where?" Blue demanded. "Where they got 'em?"

"Lot o' talk about a garden and ropes——"

"Garden? Where in hell would you find a garden in this country? You keep your eyes and ears open, Smoky! They'll let somethin' drop about the silk and where they've got Ripley. When you've got it slip up into the bluffs. I'll have someone waitin'. These gents will find me handin' out the orders around here in a day or two!"

When Blue was ready to leave, Hammersley and Itchi called him aside.

"Things have gone our way, Morgan," the professor told him. "All we have to do now is wait and be patient. A hue and cry will be raised over the disappearance of Ripley and his companions. Priest will take up the hunt for them, and he'll be urged on by my ward. We can expect to have the law called in. But nothing will come of it. In the meantime it would be wise for you to return to your place at Ute Crossing and remain there until all this blows over."

"Yeah," Blue said. "Reckon that would be a good idea." He was tempted to laugh in their faces. "You'll stick here, of course."

"Naturally!" the professor exclaimed. "It will be necessary for me to exhibit some evidence of intending to go on with the expedition. Only a matter of the utmost urgency should warrant our getting in touch for the present."

"Sure," Blue agreed. He rode away with his men, his rocky face contemptuous.

"What was the old crackpot gabbin' about?" asked Ben Ruby.

"They're figgerin' to deal us out the same way they did Brant," Morgan replied. "We're not to get in touch with him unless it's a matter of the 'utmost urgency,' he says!" He laughed mockingly. "That's rich, ain't it? They'll find we got some urgent business with 'em!"

"What are yuh headin' this way for?" Wild Bill inquired. "Ain't we goin' back to the rim?"

"We're makin' a bluff at goin' back to the Crossin'," Blue

answered. "We'll make it good enough so if they're watchin' they'll think we're on the level about it."

They were being watched, but not by the professor and Itchi. Yampa had not taken his rheumy old eyes off them. The course they took now puzzled him.

"I don't savvy this," he argued with himself. "They're movin' right along and actin' as though they was a-goin' a long piece!"

The freedom with which the men rode told the old man how their fight with Brant had gone.

"Don't even seem to figger they might run into Ripley and the little feller," Yampa muttered.

He pulled up finally and saw them disappear to the north. He didn't know what to make of it. It occurred to him that they might be returning to the Crossing, but that didn't make sense to him.

"I'll let Rip figger that one out," he decided.

Returning to the Pot Holes to pick up the partners' trail, he was surprised to find their horses still there. He knew they had expected to be back long before this. Curious, he went on to the spot below the rim where he had seen them last. Their trail was easily readable, and he followed it across the garden. He found marks of the rope in the dust. It led him to the edge of the wall, but a careful scrutiny of the cliff and river told him nothing.

"Doggone queer," he muttered. "Yuh'd think they'd got wings an' flew off of here!"

Shuffling back to the garden, he snapped to attention as he came upon the clear-cut impression of Itchi's square-toed shoe. He recognized it instantly. With the quickened interest of a bloodhound on a fresh scent he followed the peculiar footprints across the garden and off the rim. He began to backtrack on them then until he lost them around the rocks that the Nipponese had piled on the secret entrance to the cliff dwellings. It left him more bewildered than ever.

"Thet yaller varmint piled them rocks here to hide somethin'!" he growled.

Some of the boulders taxed his strength, but he managed to roll them out of the way after a lot of panting and cussing. Dropping to his knees, he dug into the loose earth with his horny hands. His grunt of disgust as he stared into the barren hole he had made was cut short by a dull thud from below that set his hair to rising. The noise was repeated and became a succession of blows as Rainbow and Darwin, battering away with heavy boulders, endeavored to split the stone that sealed the passage.

"Who are yuh there?" Yampa screeched.

"Yampa!" came the faint response. "Is that you?"

"Yeah, it shore is! What's the meanin' of all this?"

"We're trapped down here!" Rainbow answered. "Get those rocks out of the way and dig out the ground around them!"

"I got everythin' out of the way! Push or pull or do somethin' down there!"

Rainbow and Darwin put their shoulders to the slab and it slowly came up on end. Yampa's old eyes grew wider and wider as the four men crawled out, their dirt-stained faces expressing their relief and amazement at this unexpected release from death.

"Waal, you old white Injun, you shore saved our bacon!" Grumpy beamed at Yampa.

"What's down there?" the old man demanded. "An' how did a coupla smart gents like Rip and you come to let that Jap trap you thar?"

"Yampa, we'll answer all your questions as soon as we get away from here," Rainbow said tensely. "Pull those rocks back and make the place look as it did. We'll let Hammersley and Itchi think we're still down there."

It was only a matter of minutes after they left the rim before Blue and his men appeared. They stopped to water their horses and slake their thirst at the springs. They went on then, looking for Crutcher. Back at the Pot Holes Rainbow and the others waited for night to fall before attempting to reach the ranch. The partners agreed with Yampa that Blue had not returned to Ute Crossing.

"If he's busted up Brant's bunch he'll lose no time lookin'
his eyes out for the cache," Grumpy argued.

"He ain't smart enough to find it by lookin' for it," said
Yampa. The partners had told him what they had found in
the cliff dwellings. "Blue's got Smoky close to Hammersley
fer a reason. That little weasel may pick up some information. Chances are the perfessor don't know he's got a spy in
camp."

"That makes sense," Ripley admitted. "It would be like
Morgan to plant a man there. He won't get anything out of the
Jap. Hammersley is cagey too. It doesn't matter particularly
now. The marshal and his deputies will be here by tomorrow
night. I know Dan has sent for Sharp before this."

"When we get to the ranch is it your intention to keep under
cover until the marshal gets there?" asked Darwin. "I'm
thinking of Karen. I know she's alarmed at our absence already. If we don't show up by morning she'll have Priest and
his crew out looking for us. I'll be surprised if she doesn't
start out herself. She'll certainly go to the camp to inquire
about us."

"That's something to consider," said Rainbow. "I don't believe Dan would let her wander off by herself, even as far as
the camp. It goes without saying that I'm as anxious as you
to spare her any anxiety."

"I appreciate all that," Grumpy spoke up, "but you know
what's likely to happen if we show our faces around the ranch.
Ten to one Hammersley and Itchi will walk into us."

"That'll save going after them." The tall man's gray eyes
were clouded with a vague misgiving, and he could not throw
it off. He told himself he should have left Howie at the
ranch to guard Karen.

"Rip, let me understand you," Darwin said with evident
anxiety. "You couldn't arrest Hammersley in front of her.
It would tear her to pieces. You've got to think of her pride!"

"I'm thinking of her safety. I would have done well to
have thought of it last night."

Darwin's head went up and his young face drained white. "What do you mean?" he demanded.

"I mean that with Hammersley thinking he's got us out of the way, and Brant apparently washed up, there's no telling what he might try. Instead of waiting here till dark we'll start back now!"

Chapter Nineteen

THE ABSENCE of Rainbow and Darwin at breakfast that morning had brought a sharp question from Karen. Dan had tried to put her off, but when she discovered that Grumpy and Hallett were also missing she insisted on being told where they had gone.

"They didn't say where they were goin'," Priest told her. "Rip said they figgered they had found the silk. After all, that's what they're here for. The way they talked they didn't expect to be back before noon. They'll be showin' up directly."

"I can't understand Professor Darwin's going with them," she said, her anxiety unallayed.

Later in the morning, when the four men failed to return, Anne Wattress told Karen of Rainbow's unexplained interest in the cliff-dwelling sketches. "I know that he and Grumpy rode out to the camp to see Jim soon after he was talking to me," she said. "That may provide a clue."

"It does, Anne!" Karen exclaimed. "If Rainbow has found some ancient ruins and believes the silk is concealed there, he'd know Jim could help him. To leave here the way they did, late at night, and without saying anything, is proof enough they realized that what they were doing was dangerous."

Dan kept away from the house, his anxiety growing with every hour. When noon came, and there was no sign of Ripley, the rancher ordered one of his punchers to start for Vernal with instructions to wire the marshal.

Karen was waiting for Dan when he stepped in for dinner, and she had the able support of his wife.

"If yo're holding back somethin' I think it's a shame," Emmy Priest declared. "This poor girl is worried, and she has a right to be!"

"I'm a bit worried myself," admitted Dan, "but Rip and his pardner know their way around. Hallett's got some savvy too. I know Darwin couldn't be with better men. Yuh'll find they're all right, Miss Karen." He was expressing a confidence he was far from feeling. Emmy Priest knew her husband well enough to surmise as much, and she did not press him farther.

"Dan knows what he is talkin' about," she told Karen. "Rainbow is a powerful smart man. He has to be in his business. Now we won't worry any more, an' see if they ain't here for supper, hungry as orphans."

Karen pretended to give in, but she saw through their attempts to reassure her.

"If yuh go ridin' this afternoon," Dan said on the way out, "don't get out of sight of the house. I'll be away an hour or more, and I'd like to feel yuh were all right here."

"I'll be careful," promised Karen. Forty minutes later, however, driven by her mounting anxiety, she turned her pony in the direction of the camp, and it was not in her mind that she was inviting disaster. The professor and Itchi assured her that they had not seen anything of Darwin and his companions.

"Rainbow thinks he has found the stolen silk in some cliff dwellings or ruins of some sort up on the rim," she told them, her voice rising in her excitement. "It's inaccessible, I suppose. That's why Rainbow took Jim with him. If the place has a secret entrance Jim could find it. You spent some time on the rim when you were out here last, Uncle Hammersley. Did you discover anything that might help us? A prehistoric garden—soil that had been carried up there? You know so

159

much more about these things than I do. Jim says a garden is the best clue."

The professor's piercing eyes found Itchi's. The glance they exchanged had a murderous significance.

"That's all very interesting," the professor said with a patronizing laugh, "but I'm afraid it's absurd, my dear. The severity of the winters in this region would have made it impossible for the cliff dwellers to exist here. There are caverns and examples of freak erosion that Mr. Ripley might well believe were ancient ruins. I agree with you that we should make some effort to find him. We have Mr. Priest's team here. I'll have the horses put to the wagon and we shall try to reach the rim in Whirlpool Canyon. We'll begin our search there."

Having ordered Smoky to hitch the team, he stepped into his tent on the plea of getting some things. Itchi followed him.

"Miss Thane has forced the decision on us, Doctor," the latter said. "She knows far too much for our safety. When we reach the rim we shall have to contrive something. We cannot permit her to return."

Again there was perfect agreement between them.

"We shall not hesitate, my friend," the professor murmured, his hooded eyes flaming in their madness. "We know how cheap life is. See that she leaves her pony here. It will find its way back to the ranch."

Smoky eyed them with a dark, obscure interest as they drove away. The moment they were out of sight he mounted the horse Karen had left and set out to find Blue, convinced that the girl had supplied him with all the information he needed.

Back at the Cross Keys house Anne and Mrs. Priest had discovered Karen's absence.

"She's ridden out to the camp! I know it!" Emmy Priest declared nervously. "I suppose she thinks it safe enough. I wish Dan was here! He won't like it, I know!"

Priest drove in half an hour later with a load of corral poles. Emmy called him to the door at once. He didn't try to hide his annoyance when he heard that Karen had gone.

"The camp is the very place I didn't want her to go," he said. "I'll go after her right away."

Hurrying down the yard to where the crew was building a new corral, he told them to knock off work. A few minutes later they dashed away at a driving gallop.

Reaching the camp only to find it deserted stamped a deeper worry into Dan's eyes. One of the men pointed out the wagon tracks leading toward the river.

"We're goin' after 'em!" Priest told his punchers. "I hope we're in time! If we are, Hammersley and that Jap get a piece of my mind!"

Riding in a tight little group, they followed the wheel tracks without difficulty. Finally one of the men pointed out the wagon, far ahead.

"Swing around them and come up so they'll drive into us without knowin' we're waitin' for 'em!" Dan commanded. "I ain't takin' no chance with that pair!"

Itchi was driving the team and urging the horses on, but this broken country was not suited to a wagon. Finding a deep dry wash blocking the way, he was forced to turn off to his right, and when he rounded a bluff it was to drive right into the arms of the waiting men.

"Well, Mr. Priest, this is a surprise!" Hammersley called out, speaking the complete truth for once. "I suppose you are out looking for the missing men too."

"Yo're the men we're lookin' for," Dan growled. "Where yuh takin' that girl?" Karen started to reply, but Priest cut her off. "Let them answer my question!"

"Why, we were going to the rim to look for Professor Darwin——"

"Goin' to the rim in a flat-bed wagon, eh?" Dan burst out accusingly. "That's a lie on the face of it! The pair of yuh know yuh couldn't make the rim down this way! An' yo're everlastin'ly shore Rip and the others ain't to be found here!"

"You are mistaken——" Itchi started to protest.

"Shut up!" Dan rapped. "I ain't trustin' either of yuh after

161

the goin's on I've seen around here, nor am I satisfied with yore intentions toward this girl! I've sent for the marshal. I've had enough of this shootin' an' murdered men brought into my place!"

"Murdered men?" the professor inquired with a secret tightening of the throat. "To whom do you refer?"

"I'm referrin' to that bald-headed little feller who was with yore expedition! Potts, by name! He was brought in with a bullet hole in his head!"

"Why, that's impossible!" the Nipponese said with iron restraint. "Dr. Potts was drowned."

"He was murdered! Don't tell me different! Ripley had the body in my barn night before last an' brought Brant in to have a look at it!" Dan wasn't to be stopped by Karen's presence. "I helped bury the man!"

Though Itchi realized the desperateness of the situation— that their fancied security and success had been built on the quicksands of failure—his yellow face remained a stony mask. He was not ready to admit complete defeat. Devoid of fear and its hampering emotional reactions, he could think and plan even now. In some way he proposed to win free of this net that he could feel closing in on him. If to do so meant sacrificing the silk and Professor Hammersley along with it he was willing to accept those terms without scruple.

He knew the professor was of no further use to him; that almost from the beginning the man had been the weakest link in his armor. He gave him a quick glance, and sight of Thaddeus Hammersley's ashen face and fluttering hands served further warning of the rapidly approaching mental and physical collapse of the man. It sealed the professor's doom in Itchi's mind, and he told himself that any hope he entertained of escaping the consequences of these weeks of crime and intrigue depended on silencing the other quickly and forever. The next moment he had reason to believe he had waited too long already.

"Mr. Priest, I don't understand this!" the professor exclaimed. "I don't understand it at all! I didn't see Dr. Potts drown, but my assistant did. He described it to us in detail. Didn't you, Itchi?" He drew himself up accusingly. "Am I to understand that you lied to me; that you held some secret grudge against Dr. Potts and took this means of settling it?"

Hammersley's readiness to sell him out was not lost on the Japanese. He knew that fear had finally snapped his hold over the man. "That is absurd, Doctor, and you should be the first to know it," he protested eloquently. "I had only the deepest respect for Dr. Potts. I was not the only one who saw him go down——"

"Please!" Karen cried, her face bloodless with the shock of these accusations. "I insist on being heard!"

"I want you to be heard," Hammersley told her, fighting to regain his poise. "You know I am blameless——"

"No! Once I would have believed you—all my life I believed you—but no more! Ever since I first arrived in Black Forks I've felt the treachery and intrigue around me. Jim tried to warn me, and so did Rainbow. But I was blind—loyal to you—and I wouldn't listen to them. Now I know. I understand why our boat was cast adrift at the Yampa——"

"Miss Thane, you are overwrought to say such things," Itchi murmured with a spurious sympathy. "In view of the doctor's many years of devoted service to you these charges are simply fantastic. I would return to the ranch and try to calm myself if I were you. I'm sure when you and Mr. Priest —and the doctor too—have had an opportunity to think things over you will all realize how ridiculous this has been." He turned to Dan. "And you, Mr. Priest, would do well to remember that you cannot besmirch the reputation and good name of a famous man with impunity."

"That's highfalutin' language, but I ain't backin' up an inch!" Dan returned furiously, "You git up here with me, Miss Karen; we're goin' back to the house. An' when you gents get to camp leave that team hitched. I'll send out for it."

The dust of their leaving began to settle as Itchi and the professor stood there staring after them. Hammersley's thin, hawkish face was pasty. Only the eyes seemed to be alive in that tragic mask, and even their fire was dimmed.

"This is the end, my friend," he muttered heavily. "One careless step has been our undoing!"

The Japanese glared at him with a contempt that was undiluted by a drop of pity. "You have lost hold of yourself completely, Doctor," he said in stern reprimand. "Why should this be the end? What can they prove? Dr. Potts was murdered. But where is the evidence to convict us? Brant would like nothing better than to testify against us, but train robbery is a crime punishable by up to twenty years in prison. He will remember that and say nothing, nor will the others."

His iron will had lost the power to pour courage into the older man. "It's no use, my friend; we are through. If one of us can blame the other and thereby save himself it is all we can hope for now. It is your life or mine. I know you understand."

"Perfectly," was Itchi's somber answer.

When they got back to camp and Itchi found Smoky gone it removed the last reason for waiting any longer to put his plans into action. "We can thank Miss Thane's excited babbling for this," he thought. "If that man was a Morgan spy, and the fact that he has disappeared leaves little doubt of it, they will have no difficulty in finding their way into the cliff dwellings."

A surprise awaited them in the persons of the four men whom he had trapped in the ruins. Rainbow and the others would be sadly outnumbered, but Itchi had seen enough of them to be convinced that Blue and his followers would come off second best; that in a few days that tidy fortune in raw silk would be back in the possession of the railroad company.

Considering the treasure lost, the Japanese put it out of his mind. With pitiless clarity he realized that flight was all that was left to him. Seated on the edge of his cot, he turned his thoughts to fashioning some means of escape. The odds against his doing it successfully seemed prohibitive until he remembered the boat that Rainbow had left in Island Park. It was only a flimsy shell, but Itchi told himself if he could find it he would risk the river and lose himself somewhere in the lonely ninety-seven-mile stretch of Desolation Canyon. After a few weeks he could slip down through Arizona into old Mexico, find friends, and wait to see what developed. With Hammersley put beyond the possibility of talking, he believed that in a year at most he would be able to reappear in New York.

Itchi's preparations for leaving were few. He dropped an extra handful of cartridges into his pocket and took what money he had in his bag. Food and water he would need, but they could be secured later. The sun was low already. Through the flap of his tent he could see the professor slumped down moodily in a camp chair before the fire. It would have been an easy matter for Itchi to have fired a fatal shot from where he stood, but he rejected the thought. Hammersley's heart was bad. A slight strangulation would produce death and leave no marks. Whoever found him under such circumstances would very likely believe he had died a natural death.

Itchi was familiar with the methods of the footpads who plied their trade along the water fronts of his native Osaka and Nagasaki. They invariably applied the garrote to their victims. Taking a large silk handkerchief, he turned in the ends and rolled it into a rope. Tying a slipknot in one end, he led the other end through it. It was an innocent-looking weapon, its deadliness depending on how long and with what force its pressure was put against a man's throat.

The professor did not look up as he heard the Japanese approaching. Itchi spoke to him. "You are brooding, Doctor, and there is no need for it. This moment calls for courage, not regrets."

The professor nodded. "Do not imagine that I have been sitting here pitying myself. Long ago we agreed that sentiment had no place in our lives."

"Precisely."

"But you have been as my right hand to me, and now it becomes necessary to amputate that hand. It is not easy, my

165

friend, but there is no other way. You will understand that it is not what I wish."

"It is not what either of us wishes that matters." Itchi's tone was deceivingly soft as he stepped up behind the professor. "It is necessity that drives the bargain now. You have made your decision, and I have made mine."

The professor caught a note of danger in that soft tone. He straightened, a question on his lips, and as his head came up Itchi dropped his silken noose over it and drew the ends tight. Thaddeus Hammersley's last question ended in a strangled gasp. A convulsive shudder shook him briefly, then he became a limp, dead weight.

Itchi waited until he was convinced the man had ceased to breathe. Removing the noose, then, he settled the professor back in his chair.

"I am sorry, Doctor," he murmured. "It was either one or the other of us. You could not hope to save yourself, but you may be able to save me."

A canteen of water and a small package of food were readily available. With an apologetic bow to the dead man Itchi left camp then and set out for the bluffs. The tracks he found in the dust, a mile to the north, told him nothing, though they had been made within the last half-hour and marked the course of Rainbow's return to the Cross Keys. At that very moment the partners with Darwin and Howie were riding into the ranch yard. Before they could get down from their saddles Mrs. Priest and Anne ran out to give them the news.

Rainbow's face whipped tight, and he was about to speak when a cry from Grumpy swung him around. The little one pointed out a group of riders who had just topped a low rise to the east.

"That's Dan now, Rainbow! They got the girl with 'em!"

A glad cry escaped Darwin and he wanted to ride out to meet them. Ripley held him back.

"They'll be here in a few minutes, Jim," he advised. "Chances are Karen's had all the excitement she can stand.

Have the women get her into the house as soon as you can. If she asks about us I'll tell her we found the silk and forget the rest of it for the present."

"Jim, you're all right! And you, Rainbow! All of you!" Karen cried. The moment Dan lifted her down she ran to Darwin. His strong arms drew her close. When she looked up her eyes were wet and shining. "I was so worried about you! I just seemed to go all to pieces. . . . You found the silk?"

"Yes." Darwin nodded. "Rainbow had the right hunch."

Karen's eyes went to Ripley. "You know how it got there, of course. I guess we all do. It's been a terrible shock to me. I . . . I——" Her voice broke and she couldn't go on.

"We won't say any more now," Rainbow murmured. He jerked his head for Darwin to take her into the house. Anne and Mrs. Priest went with them. He turned then for an explanation from Dan.

Handing his horse over to one of his men, Priest walked across to the blacksmith shop with the partners and Howie. "Mebbe I said more than I should," he began. "But I couldn't help it. When I found her, Hammersley and the Jap had her half way to those badlands along Whirlpool Canyon. Their story that they was out lookin' for yuh was more'n I could stand. I knew they had the girl there to do her harm, so I shot my mouth off plenty."

"Just what did you say?" Rainbow demanded, tight-lipped.

Dan repeated what he had said to the professor and Itchi. "The girl got it, and they couldn't lie out of it to her. I don't know all the details, but I can put it together good enough. On the way in I told her just what was what. So she knows where she stands. It didn't break her up so bad as you might think. Seems she's been doin' some figgerin' for herself."

"She certainly had to be told; it couldn't be kept back much longer," Rainbow acknowledged. "How did Hammersley and the Jap take it?"

"It floored the old man. I thought Itchi got a little white

around the gills too. When do yuh figger Sharp will show up?"

"I don't know," replied Ripley. "But I won't wait for him. We'll ride out to the camp this evening and take that pair into custody. I've got a shut-and-closed case against them as far as the robbery goes. It will be the marshal's job to round up Brant's bunch. The rest of us will go after Blue."

"I reckon that's the program," Grumpy muttered. He wasn't too happy about it. "Things ain't worked out the way I figgered. I thought we'd git Morgan dead to rights. That's the only way to git him if you don't want him to slip through yore fingers."

"I'll take a chance that we can establish his connection with Hammersley," decided Rainbow. "We can always tie that freight wreck on him. That would keep him out of circulation for a few years."

Karen did not come down to supper. Jim said she was trying hard to pull herself together.

"It will take her a year to get over this," he said. "Her life has been torn up by the roots."

"I'd get her away from this country in a day or two," advised Rainbow. "A new environment will help her to get a grip on herself."

"Karen is young, and she has a lot of courage," Anne remarked. "She may surprise you."

They were still at the table when the sharp thud of running horses reached them. A few minutes later a band of riders dashed into the yard at a furious pace.

Grumpy was the first to reach the door. "It's Brant!" was his startled cry. He had half expected to find Blue Morgan there in a surprise attack. "They look as though they'd had the pants shot off 'em!"

Brant pulled his horse to a slithering stop. "Where's Ripley?" he yelled.

"Right here," Rainbow answered for himself. "What's on your mind?"

"You see the shape we're in," growled Brant. "Morgan's got us outnumbered six to one. He must have thirty men with him. He's been turning us back all day. I made up my mind to square one thing with Hammersley and the Jap before it was too late. You were right about Potts. Itchi killed him on the old man's orders. They wanted to get the girl too. They had that all cooked up back in New York."

Ripley and Grumpy exchanged an understanding glance. They knew from what Yampa had told them that it couldn't be Morgan who was closing in on these men. There was only one other solution, and the little one was quick to grasp it.

"It's Sharp!" he muttered under his breath. "He ain't waited at Mormon Valley!"

A warning cry from Ginger Revell cut across what he was saying. Brant swung his horse around, but in every direction he looked he could see horsemen closing in on the yard.

"Keep your hands away from your guns" Rainbow commanded. "Start reaching! You gents have come to the end of your string. This ain't Morgan riding in. It's Asa Sharp and his deputies!"

Chapter Twenty

ASA SHARP loped into the Cross Keys yard, gray with the dust of the day's riding. Perched high on a big black horse, he looked dumpier than ever, his legs too short and his round, pink-cheeked face somehow suggesting a pleasant, mild-mannered character out of *Snow White and the Seven Dwarfs*. The illusion died the moment he spoke.

"Get their guns and put the irons on 'em, boys!" he told two of his deputies. "This makes it a clean sweep! Much obliged to you, Rip! We picked up four of this gang about twenty miles west of here shortly after daylight. Some of the boys are bringing them in. The whole pack of 'em was trying to leave the country." He turned to Priest. "Dan, can I have the use of your barn till morning for my men and these prisoners?"

"Shore," Dan agreed. "Help yoreself!"

"Say, what's the arrest for?" demanded Brant hotly.

"Come, come, Brant!" Sharp grumbled. "After fourteen hours in the saddle, dodging lead and eating your dust, I'm in no mood for humor. That little affair at Green River Bridge is what you're being arrested for. Take 'em away, boys!"

The marshal slipped down from his horse and marched up to the gallery where Emmy Priest stood.

"Why, Mr. Sharp!" she exclaimed, beaming a welcome.

Sharp pumped her hand. "I got a big bunch of men with me, Emmy. They got rations with 'em, so I won't ask you to feed 'em." His voice dropped confidentially. "I'm afraid you'll have to make an exception of me, though. You suppose you could beat up a batch of biscuit and fry me three or four eggs?"

"I shore can!" Emmy laughed. "I'll call yuh when I'm ready."

Sharp took a seat on the gallery with the partners and Priest.

"I had Dan send for you this noon," Rainbow informed him.

The marshal caught the question that wasn't asked. "It's all right, Rip; I wasn't breaking my promise to you. I stuck close to Mormon Valley until day before yesterday. I got to thinking that if either Brant or Morgan tried to run out there'd be nothing to stop 'em, with me stuck up there. I moved down across the Uinta so I could keep the back door shut. I had no intention of barging in on you until we ran into gunfire."

The explanation satisfied Rainbow. "It's worked out all right," he said. "Grump and I were going to ride out to Hammersley's camp and take him and the Japanese into custody tonight. We better do it. When you've had a bite to eat, the three of us will go after them."

"If you're ready for that, things must have been going your way. Suppose you set me right."

Rainbow gave him a detailed account of what had transpired since they parted at Green River Bridge.

"That's fine!" Asa declared. "You couldn't have done better. I thought you were taking on a pretty big order by yourselves, but you seem to have got away with it. You and Grumpy haven't left much for me to do."

"Don't be too sure o' that," the fiery little man growled. "Blue's still on the loose, an' he don't play for fun."

Sharp disavowed any intention of underestimating Morgan. "He'll fight to the finish when he's cornered. But he's never been up against anything like this, Grump. He knows this wild, broken country on both sides of the river, and it's always suited his game. He may be able to play hide-and-seek with us for a time, but if he ever tries to break away he'll find he's caught in a ring of law officers. The Federal marshals of Colorado have the way blocked in that direction, and there's another big force strung out along the Denver and Rio Grande to the south."

Mrs. Priest called the marshal in, and through the window Grumpy observed him doing ample justice to her biscuits and bacon and eggs. A few minutes later Howie and Darwin came down the gallery.

"The three of yuh goin' out there alone, or do yuh want some help?" Howie asked.

"We can handle it," said Rainbow. "The two of you stick here."

Soon after Sharp stepped out of the house he and the partners rode off. From a distance they could see that the Hammersley camp was in darkness.

"Looks deserted," Grumpy muttered when they were only a hundred yards away. "Be fine if they've pulled out on us."

"Hammersley's here," Rainbow said. "Over there by the fire, just beyond the big tent."

171

The fire had burned down to smoldering coals, but its faint glow revealed the professor seated in his camp chair.

"He seems to be here alone," Sharp observed, his tone apprehensive. "We may be riding into something."

"You get Hammersley," suggested Rainbow. "We'll look for the Jap and Smoky Yeager."

"Right," the marshal grunted. Stepping down from his saddle, he walked over to the fire and made himself known. "The jig is up, Hammersley. You know why we're here. You're under arrest! Get up and let me see if you've got a gun on you."

The professor continued to stare back at him with unseeing eyes. Sharp started to speak again, only to check himself abruptly. Hastily he threw a clump of dead sage on the fire. As it broke into flame a startled cry escaped him.

"Rip!" the marshal yelled. "Come here—quick!" And when Rainbow came running: "Look here This man's dead!"

"And he's been dead for several hours," said Rainbow. He called to Grumpy.

"They ain't around," the little one told him. "Dan's team is here, but the pony the girl was ridin' is gone." He stopped as he caught sight of the lifeless body of the professor. "Waal!" he grunted. "Kicked out, eh? Don't seem to be a mark on him."

"It may have been his heart," said Sharp. "He's got that look about him."

Rainbow reserved his opinion. With Grumpy's help he carried Hammersley into his tent and placed him on a cot. When a lamp had been lighted he knelt down and made a careful examination of the body. A faint welt on the neck of the dead man caught his attention.

"I guess that's the answer to this," he remarked. "I'd say this man was strangled to death."

"It was the Jap," muttered Grumpy. "Couldn't have been anybody else. Blue or one of his bunch would have used a gun."

They searched Itchi's tent and found nothing, but a few

172

minutes later Rainbow, fishing in the fire, found the knotted end of the silk handkerchief the Nipponese had used. Sharp took possession of it.

"What would you say was the reason for this, Rip?" Asa asked.

"I don't know; your guess would be as good as mine. Dan told me Hammersley seemed to go all to pieces when he faced him down this afternoon. Maybe that's the reason the Jap killed him, figuring it was too dangerous to string along with him any further."

"I reckon that's about the way it was," the little man agreed. "It's a cinch Mr. Itchi is takin' it on the run. Him and Smoky may have left here together. If we find Morgan we'll most likely find the Jap."

Ripley shook his head. "I doubt it. We know one of that pair left here on foot. That most likely was Itchi. When Karen came here early in the afternoon and spoke her mind Yeager learned all he wanted. I imagine he pulled out as soon as they were out of sight."

Sharp nodded. "That makes sense to me, but why are you so sure the Jap hasn't joined up with Morgan?"

"He's too cunning, Asa. He's thinking of saving his hide now. That's why he killed Hammersley. By himself, he figures he can slip out of this country."

"Well, he'll never make it!" Sharp said with quiet emphasis. "It may take a few days, but we'll turn him up. He'll be recognized wherever he shows his face; there're no Japs in this part of Utah. I'm going to forget about it for the present and go after Blue. I've got more men than I need. I'll send three or four into Vernal with Brant's bunch, first thing in the morning, and then we'll try to pick up Morgan's trail. It would only be tossing away lives for nothing to attempt it tonight."

They were ready to leave a few minutes later.

"You better have one of your men send down an undertaker from town," Rainbow suggested to the marshal. "He can take both Potts and Hammersley back with him. If you'll

173

drive the team in for Dan, Grump, it will save him sending for it."

Asa Sharp was a taciturn, unemotional man as a rule, but the passing of Thaddeus Hammersley under such circumstances rested heavily on him. "It's a terrible way for a man of his prominence to end up," he said to Rainbow. "Tossing everything away on a mad venture of this sort is hard to understand. It couldn't have been only the money or wanting to get rid of the girl. The man must have been mad."

"That would seem to be the answer," Ripley said and offered no further comment. At the ranch he left it to Sharp to explain to Dan and Howie why they were returning alone and walked aside with Darwin.

"I'm glad it ended this way," Jim said when he had been told that the professor was dead. "A trial would have been a ghastly experience for Karen. Will either of us be needed as witnesses?"

"I see no reason why you should," Rainbow answered. He told Darwin the body would be removed to town the next day. "I wouldn't let Karen know anything about it until it's all over. I suppose we'll be pulling away pretty early in the morning. I can't say how long we'll be gone. If you and Karen leave before I get back tell her good-bye for me."

"I'm afraid she wouldn't go that way, Rip. I 'wouldn't either. If we're not here we'll be at the hotel in Vernal."

Half an hour before dawn Sharp had his men up. A bite to eat and getting his prisoners started for town did not take long. By the time the sun was above the bluffs to the east the posse was headed for the river. The partners and Howie rode with the marshal, and they were confident of success. When they reached the bluffs, Sharp divided his forces.

"You take three of my men, Rip; that'll make you six strong. Swing north and come out at the river at the lower end of Missionary Run. Start working south then. I'll give Vinson an equal number with which to hold this line. I'll take the rest and circle off to the south. We'll meet tonight on the rim at the head of Whirlpool Canyon. If we don't have any luck we'll try the same tactics farther down tomorrow."

He named the men who were to go with Rainbow.

"There's just one thing more," the marshal said as they were ready to part. "Don't take any foolish chances. If you draw some shots, drop back and hold your ground until the rest of us can join you. That's all!"

The three groups soon lost sight of one another.

"Asa knows his business," Grumpy remarked, "but there're holes in this net. It'd take a hundred men to stop up all of 'em."

"There's a lot of country to cover," Rainbow agreed. "We've got an ace in the hole in Yampa. I suspect we'll be seeing something of him before the day is over."

It was a hope that was not realized. Not only did they fail to see anything of the old man, but they found no trace of Morgan's crowd. When they met the marshal and Pete Vinson on the rim that evening they learned that the others had met with no better luck.

Sharp refused to be discouraged. "We'll do better tomorrow. Blue won't quit this country."

"I don't know about that," argued Grumpy. "If by chance Itchi's with him he knows how things stand. That bein' the case, he'll play tag with us. I don't see no point in chasin' him by day if we're goin' to give him a chance to slip back past us by night."

"Neither do I," Sharp said without rancor. "What do you suggest?"

"Spreadin' out in a line east and west an' holdin' it till daylight."

The marshal turned to Rainbow. "You got anything better to offer?"

"No. That would be my suggestion too."

Sharp gave the necessary orders and the posse spread out for the night. The move failed to bring results. Worse still, the following day proved as fruitless as the first.

Asa Sharp's complacency had fled completely when they met for the evening rendezvous.

"If they were on the move we'd have cut a fresh trail by now," he grumbled, smarting with defeat. "You didn't see anything of Yampa Jackson either?"

"Not a glimpse," replied Rainbow. "He may be dead. If Blue ran into him he'd know what the old man was doing down here, and he wouldn't hesitate a second about rubbing him out. It's getting plain enough to me that Morgan is holed up somewhere."

"Now yo're talkin'!" Grumpy cried, hopping to his feet excitedly. "We haven't looked in the spot they're most likely to be. I mean them cliff dwellin's! Itchi could have told 'em, er they could have found their way there by themselves!"

"That may be it, Rip!" said Sharp. "That may be the answer to this puzzle! They'd figure we wouldn't look there. From what you tell me they'll be hard to get at if that's where they're forted up."

"It's an idea," agreed Rainbow. "We'll have a look, but this is one job that'll need daylight. We'll move up tonight and have a try at it first thing in the morning."

They reached the position they wanted just about midnight. The horses were as weary as the men. Rainbow had a look at the garden from a distance. In the moonlight it appeared unchanged. He turned in then and had been asleep for almost four hours when Grumpy tugged violently at his blanket.

"Wake up, Rip" the little one whispered excitedly. "Howie and me snuck down to the garden. The trap is standin' wide open!"

"You're sure of that?"

" 'Course we're sure!" Hallett confirmed. "They're down there!"

The sleeping men began to sit up. Sharp pulled on his boots hurriedly. "Be stirring, boys!" he ordered tensely. "It'll be light enough to see in a few minutes! You go ahead, Rip. We'll follow you!"

Rainbow found the stone slab over the secret entrance to the ruins standing on end just as Grumpy and Hallett had said. The marshal crawled up beside him. Down in the passage they saw only inky blackness.

"Drop back a few yards and keep this spot covered," Asa told the men. "When there's some light down there I'll try it."

"It'll be suicide if you do!" Grumpy growled.

"That goes with the job," returned Asa.

Finally a glimmer of dawn touched the stone stairway. Sharp lowered his head and reached for the first step with his short legs. Rainbow and Grumpy followed close behind him.

The withering fusillade they expected did not come, and the other men began to stream down the stairs. Within a few minutes all were below.

"They ain't here!" the marshal rasped. "If they were they wouldn't have let us get this far!"

Staring in awe at the ancient, crumbling ruins, the possemen crawled through the openings that led from one apartment to the next, guns ready for an ambush.

"I don't know how else to explain the entrance being open," Rainbow remarked.

A yell from Grumpy swung them around sharply.

"Rip! Asa" the little one cried. "Come here! The silk's gone! Ain't a bale of it left!"

Chapter Twenty-one

INVESTIGATION confirmed the fact that the silk had disappeared from its hiding place. Asa Sharp puffed out his cheeks and worked himself into a rage.

"I don't want to say I told you so," Grumpy muttered

pointedly, "but I figgered there might be a slip 'twixt the cup an' the lip. The silk's gone, an' so are Morgan and the Jap, an' that pat hand we thought we was holdin' turns out to be just a couple of pairs and a joker."

Sharp stopped his worried pacing to whirl on them fiercely. "What about Yampa Jackson?" he whipped out. "Does this explain why you haven't seen anything of him for two days? Has he sold you out?"

Rainbow shook his head. "You can forget that, Asa. I took a chance on Yampa, and he came through. I know how lawless he is, but he didn't have anything to do with this. You'll find it was Blue. The silk is gone, and that's as tough a break for us as it is for you. The thing to do now is find it. When we do it's my guess we'll find Morgan too."

"That's good advice, if you know where to start looking," Sharp said testily. "Where did Morgan get horses enough to cart all that stuff away?"

"I don't believe he used horses. Those bales were never taken up the stairs. Blue can't have over eight or nine men, and some of them are pretty badly shot up. He had to find an easy way of moving the silk."

"You mean he had boats?" Grumpy demanded incredulously.

"No, I believe he just dumped the silk into the river and took a chance that the bales would hold together when they struck the water. The way they are wrapped they're almost waterproof; they'd float for a few hours, and the current would take them a long way in that time. If I'm right there'll be some proof of it here."

A careful examination showed unmistakable traces of where the tightly packed bales had been moved to the very edge of the bench. Grumpy gathered up a little ball of jute fibers that had been rubbed off the wrappings.

"That means Island Park," the little one volunteered. "No use lookin' this side of the islands!"

Sharp started for the stairs at once. "We're wastin' our time here," he said gruffly. "Let's be moving!"

178

Striking south on the rim, they had gone less than a mile when they saw a gaunt figure riding toward them, his pants flapping about his spindly shanks.

"Hold up!" Rainbow yelled at Sharp. "Here's Yampa!"

"Waal, where in the name o' sin have yuh been hidin'?" the old man screeched angrily. "I bin lookin' for yuh since last evenin'! Morgan's down in the islands, an' that bunch o' sidewinders has been fishin' them silk bales out o' the river for hours!"

Remembering the long ago when Sharp had chased him up and down eastern Utah on several occasions, Yampa eyed the marshal with unconcealed hostility. Asa caught the look.

"Don't go shying away from me," he said brusquely. "I haven't anything on my mind as far as you're concerned. Suppose you tell us all you know. How did you happen to spot Blue?"

"If it's just the same to yuh, I'll do my talkin' to Rip," the old man muttered stubbornly. Without further bickering he told Rainbow how he had followed Smoky Yeager and had seen him meet Morgan. They had got away from him then, and he had next encountered them the following afternoon, moving to the south as rapidly as the going would permit.

"I didn't know what was up, but it was plain enough they was high-tailin' it about sumpin'. . . . How did that silk get into the river?"

"They tossed it in, Yampa. They got into the cliff dwellings. Are they still in the park?"

"Yep, an' workin' like beavers. They found a duckboat that some feller left there. Blue got in it and snagged the bales as they come driftin' down. I figgered they'd try to hide the stuff on one of the islands. But not them! Yuh know where the three small mesas are on the way west toward the San Blas chalk cliffs?"

"Yeah."

"Waal, that's where they're packin' it away. On the highest one! Must be a big cup up there. Yuh'd never guess they was anythin' there at all."

"Is Itchi with them?" Rainbow asked, impatience to be off roughening his voice.

"That yaller punkin'? No! Has he turned up missin'?"

"I'll tell you the answer as we ride along," said Rainbow. "Let's go, Asa! We couldn't ask for a better break!"

"You said it!" Sharp growled. "If we grab Morgan with the stolen silk in his possession he'll never beat this case!"

Asa Sharp was no stranger to Island Park. By the time he reached the trail that Rainbow and Grumpy had used between the islands and the Cross Keys he had his plans completed. He told the men what he wanted.

"I'll give you plenty of time to get in position. I'll be off to the west. Look that way. I'll tie my handkerchief on a stick and wave it when I think we're ready. It would be a waste of breath to ask Morgan's bunch to give themselves up. When you get my signal start banging away, and keep it up until they give some sign of being willing to quit."

The possemen rode away to form their circle.

"You fellers come with me," Yampa told the partners and Hallett. "This is a showdown I been waitin' for, an' I aim to be up in the front row!"

"Yo're gittin' so you chatter like an old woman," Grumpy railed at him. "Shut up an' lead the way!"

About half an hour later Yampa reined in sharply. "Take a look down there!" he ordered.

"By Christopher, they're still here!" Grumpy burst out grimly. "If they try to bust away from Sharp this is the way they'll come!"

"We're strong enough to stop them," said Rainbow, watching the two men Blue had posted on top of the mesa raising the bales by ropes and stowing them away. The work was almost finished. "Suppose we cross this draw and get in a little closer," he suggested. "It will be some time before Asa is ready."

A minute later, however, a rifle cracked. Blue was not being caught napping. He had got a glimpse of one of Sharp's deputies and snapped a shot at him instantly. That shot was returned with interest. The number of rifles in action seemed to convince Blue that discretion was the better part of valor. With a cry to his men, he reached his horse and led them up the slope where Rainbow and the others waited. Yampa didn't hesitate. His gun barked, and Blue's hat sailed away.

"My shootin's gittin' terrible!" the old man growled. Before he could fire a second time Morgan had veered off. In a second or two the outlaw and his men had dropped out of sight behind a stringer of rock where they were temporarily safe. From that protection they set their guns to bucking.

"Move over a few yards!" Rainbow ordered. "We'll smoke 'em out of there!" He could see the posse closing in on three sides.

"There go their hosses!" Grumpy called out. "We got 'em high and dry now!"

Trying to improve the advantage of their new position, they moved out still farther, only to find they had exposed themselves. It brought a quick blast from below. Hallett's gun went flying from his hands, and he rolled over groaning. "Shoulder," he muttered, gritting his teeth. Down below, Pete Vinson, Sharp's chief deputy, went tumbling out of his saddle. But two of Morgan's small force were also down, and a slug from Grumpy's rifle slapped into Ben Ruby and sent him spinning.

Ten minutes later Sharp and four of his men got around in back of the ledge and had the trapped men at their mercy. It didn't take Blue long to realize the folly of continuing the fight. A glancing bullet had laid his cheek open, and it was a bloody face that he turned to the marshal when he stepped out, hands raised in surrender.

"It took enough of you, didn't it?" he snarled when he saw the number of men in the posse. Sight of old Yampa threw him into an even more violent rage. "It's easy to see that you've been ratting on me or you wouldn't be riding with this bunch!"

"I shore been settin' on yore tail, Blue," Yampa cackled.

"Yuh want to take a long look at this country. Yuh won't be seein' it ag'in for a few years!"

Morgan tried to break away from the two men who were holding him and fling himself at Yampa.

"Forget it, Blue!" Rainbow rapped. "You've been playing with a stacked deck ever since you wrecked that freight at Split Mountain. I advise you to call up that sense of humor of yours. You're going to need it."

Sharp came over and called Rainbow aside. "One dead and seven wounded—a couple pretty bad," he said.

"Who was killed?"

"Smoky Yeager. I'm going to leave a few men here to guard the silk and get the rest started for the Cross Keys and on into town. When I get that done I'll set out with you and Grumpy and see if we can't get a line on where that Jap is hiding."

"Yampa will go with us," Rainbow told him. "He's a good tracker. And I wish you'd have someone wire Moran how things have gone."

"Sure," Asa agreed. When he had the wounded and the prisoners moving away with their escort he came back to the partners. "This is a good day's work," he declared simply. "I don't take any credit for it; that all goes to you. It will take a few days to freight the silk out. That'll about wind things up down here."

"They won't be wound up as far as I'm concerned until we've put a pair of handcuffs on the Jap," said Rainbow soberly. "Right from scratch he's been headman behind all this business."

"Them's my sentiments," Grumpy seconded. "He can't be far away. I'll give him credit for bein' smart enough to take a canteen of water with him when he quit camp, but that won't last him forever. If we watch them springs up on the rim we'll be pretty shore to see him afore long."

"You boys ain't got no argument with me," Sharp declared. "I want Itchi as bad as you do, and I'll stick with you until we get him if it takes a year."

182

Though he possessed but a scanty knowledge of this wild country, Saburo Itchi had successfully dodged the posse for two days and reached Island Park, only to find Morgan and his gang there. The use to which the duckboat in which he hoped to make his escape was being put left him in no doubt as to what had happened.

He wasted no time on self-recrimination or regret. It was a source of some satisfaction to him, however, to realize that Blue Morgan could not hope to profit by his undertaking. Months of careful planning, of looking after every detail, had gone into the robbing of the Silk Express. The stolen silk had been concealed in the one place that promised security. If such a superbly calculated and executed effort had failed, how could Morgan, with his low, fumbling mind, hope to win out? In a few days at most the silk would be out of the outlaw's hands and in the possession of the law.

It was in Itchi's mind to make sure of that, to get word to Sharp and the partners. The desire became so overwhelming that he considered it even at cost of his own safety. It was a sacrifice he was not called on to make, however, for on the third day he saw the posse closing in. He waited no longer. Turning back north, he followed the rim, being careful to keep to the hard rock where his stubby feet left no trail that could be followed. The food and water he had taken from the camp were still almost untouched. With care they would last a week to ten days. After that he could go a week without food if necessary. When Hammersley and he had discovered the cliff dwellings they had explored them thoroughly. Itchi knew Rainbow would look for him there, but he believed he could secrete himself and remain hidden until they had given up trying to find him. Win or lose, it was now his best chance, and he did not hesitate about embracing it.

When he was beyond sound of the gunfire in Island Park the Japanese quickened his pace, and before noon he was in sight of the old garden. Removing his shoes, he reached the open entrance. He did not make the mistake of closing it.

Gun drawn against any surprise that might await him, he descended to the ruins.

The partners, Asa Sharp, and old Yampa were there a couple of hours later. Yampa covered the ground about the entrance carefully but failed to find any fresh tracks.

They found the ruins apparently as deserted as when they had seen them last. An hour's fruitless searching gave them no reason to change their minds about it.

"He ain't here; that's all there is to it," said the marshal. "Is it your idea to go back above and wait out around here for a day or two on the chance that he'll show up?" he asked Ripley.

"No need of all four of us waiting. I'll stick here. The rest of you start swinging through the bluffs. You come in this evening if you don't pick the Jap up before then."

They were about to climb the stairs when Yampa let out a surprised whistle. He had found the clearcut imprint of a stockinged foot in the dust.

"I was right after all," Grumpy muttered guardedly. "He's in here somewhere!"

The others nodded.

"Some secret room that we don't know about," said Rainbow. "Keep your guns ready. That little rat will open up on us if we get close to him."

With nerves taut they went through the ruins again, expecting a shot at every step. Only a silence of the dead rewarded them.

"Jim Darwin's the man to help us out now," Rainbow declared when they had returned to the stairs. "We could be here forever and not find the secrets of this place. Yampa, you fork your bronc and go to the ranch. Bring Darwin back with you. And don't spare your horse getting there."

"Shall I bring Dan along?"

"No, just Darwin. And don't do any loose talking that will alarm the womenfolks."

Waiting was slow work. The hours seemed to drag by.

"A stick of dynamite would open things up in a hurry," Grumpy grumbled.

"That's not a bad idea," Sharp chimed in, but Rainbow refused to consider it.

"These old ruins have some scientific value," he said. "It would be nothing short of vandalism to destroy them. We've got the Jap penned up, and if we have to we'll wait here and starve him out."

The afternoon was half gone when Yampa arrived with Jim.

"No," the latter said in answer to Rainbow's question. "In my experience with cliff dwellings I have never found any secret rooms. Of course there's the priests' room below the *estufa*—it's really a dungeon, where they repaired to do penance. Have you looked in it?"

"No. We didn't know about it."

"That's likely where we'll find him. If you'll keep the trap covered I'll open it."

"When you get it open drop back at once," Rainbow told him. "That little sidewinder's got a gun on him, and he'll use it."

They made their way to the circular *estufa*. Itchi heard them coming and recognized Darwin's muffled voice. He knew why Jim had been sent for; that in a few minutes he would be discovered and caught without a chance of escape. Death was a price he had always been prepared to pay for failure, and he did not flinch at it now, but he was determined to make it costly for the two men he held responsible for his predicament. The crumbling masonry offered no great resistance to the blade of his knife. He had already made an opening in the wall so that he might have better air. He turned to it now and in a few seconds had lifted a stone out of place. A second one followed, and as Darwin slowly lifted the trap in the ceiling of the dungeon Itchi crawled through the wall and reached the next apartment.

Yampa stood only a few feet away. Itchi crashed into him and bowled him over. The old man's startled cry brought

185

the others on the run. Grumpy was in time to see the Japanese disappear through an opening. He slapped a shot at him without effect.

Itchi had reached a point of vantage, and as the four men tried to close in he emptied his gun at them.

"Keep down!" Rainbow yelled as the slugs whined over their heads. "Rush him when he stops to reload!"

He was the first to follow his own advice, and when he heard Itchi's gun click on an empty shell he leaped up and covered the ten feet to the opening in a bound.

Seeing Rainbow hurtling toward him, Itchi flung his useless gun at the detective's head. It struck the latter a glancing blow, but it did not stop him.

The force of Rainbow's rush carried both of them to the floor. Over and over they rolled, and Ripley's gun was knocked out of his hand. He tried to get his arms free, but the Japanese held them securely pinned and rolled him over again. He recognized that this was the end for him, and he proposed to take Rainbow with him. The edge of the shelf, with its sheer drop of almost two thousand feet to the river, was only inches away.

Rainbow realized the man's intention and fought to break free. The next second Grumpy flung himself on them and his gun barrel crashed against Itchi's skull.

"Great Christopher!" the little one gasped. "He was all set to take you over, Rainbow! Another second and he would have done it!"

Sharp came up panting excitedly, and snapped the manacles on the Nipponese. "Drag him back!" he growled. "I don't want that treacherous pup to cheat the law!"

Rainbow picked himself up. There was a smear of blood on his forehead.

"Clipped you a little when he threw that gun at you," Grumpy muttered.

"Almost floored me," Rainbow admitted. "It don't amount to anything though. Let's get him out of here and on his way to Vernal in a hurry. Suppose you and Jim drag him up the stairs."

When they had Itchi up above they carried him to the springs and doused him with water. In a few minutes he opened his eyes.

"Don't show me them teeth!" Grumpy growled at him. "Yo're ridin' on a one-way ticket this time, mister! Get up on yore legs and don't let a peep out of you if you don't want to feel the barrel of this gun ag'in!"

Rainbow had walked aside with the marshal. "He's your prisoner, Asa. Grumpy and I will be in Vernal tomorrow. We'll see you there. When you lock this fellow up don't put him in a cell alone. He'll hang himself if you do."

"I'll take care of him," Sharp promised gruffly. "He'll go to trial if I know it. I guess we can go."

Rip spoke to Yampa. "You can head north from here," he told the old man. "You go back to the Crossing. We'll see you there in a few days. I told you the railroad company would take care of you, and I'll see that they do."

"O.K." Yampa grinned. He flung a leg over his saddle. "I'll be lookin' for yuh," he called back as he rode off.

The partners, Asa Sharp, and Jim Darwin reached the ranch with Itchi in the late afternoon. The prisoner had not offered a word. With frozen, contemptuous eyes he regarded them.

Riding into the yard, they were surprised to see Tom Moran step off the gallery to greet them. The railroad man was equally surprised at sight of the Japanese.

"I came down to congratulate you boys and the marshal," he said to Rainbow. "Apparently you've made a clean sweep."

"It worked out just about the way I promised you it would. I suppose you've talked with Asa's deputies."

"Yes. They told me about the silk and all the rest of it. I'm not going to try to thank you, but if you'll drop in on me at Platte City next week I'll hand you something a little more tangible than words of appreciation."

They talked for a few minutes. Rainbow mentioned Yampa and Moran agreed to reward the old man. Sharp was anxious to be on his way with his prisoner.

"I'll ride up with you," Tom offered. He got his horse, and after a word or two rode off with the marshal and Itchi. Rainbow went on to the house. Emmy Priest was there alone.

"Miss Thane isn't around?" Rainbow asked, sober-voiced.

"No, thank goodness. Dan has the girls out with him. They'll be back for supper." Emmy shook her head over the capture of the Japanese. "I suppose a body should have sympathy even for such as he, but I don't feel none for him, Rainbow. I never liked him from the moment I laid eyes on him."

Rip sat in the kitchen, talking to her for some time. It was a pleasant spot, with its spicy odors and promise of good things to come. But he was not merely killing time; he was trying to reach a decision, and he made it at last.

"I reckon it's time for me and the little fellow to be pulling away," he said. "Did Tom Moran square up the bill?"

"Twice over!" Emmy exclaimed apologetically. "Yuh know I didn't want to take nothin'. Dan and me was just glad to have yuh here. We'll miss yuh. . . . Perfessor Darwin's takin' Karen to California. They're goin' to be married. That gets a girl's mind off her troubles. At least fer a time," she added. "I suppose he told yuh."

"No . . . but that's fine," Rainbow murmured, his mouth suddenly tight. "I'm glad for them." He glanced at his watch, though the kitchen clock had just struck five. Getting up, he went to the door. Across the yard he could see Grumpy gassing with one of Dan's punchers. Rainbow called to him to fetch up the horses.

"Say your good-byes, Grump," he advised. "We're leaving."

Emmy wasn't as blind as she pretended. "Yuh ain't goin' without sayin' good-bye to her, are yuh?" she demanded reprovingly.

"It will be better," Rainbow said soberly. "Jim can tell her the news about the Jap. You might mention to her that if she

188

ever wants to get in touch with me, a letter in care of Judge Carver at Black Forks will do it."

He went upstairs and gathered his few belongings into a saddlebag. Coming down, he found Karen standing in the living room, waiting for him. They were alone for a moment.

"Emmy says you are leaving," Karen murmured, her eyes searching his. "I didn't think you would run away from me, You know how much I admire you. I . . . I owe my life to you, Rainbow——"

The tall man shook his head. "You don't owe me anything, Karen. I'm sorry I couldn't do more for you. I understand that Jim and you are going to California—that you're to be married soon. I'm glad for both of you." His smile was unconsciously wistful. It rubbed the hardness out of his mouth. "I . . . I envy him."

He reached out to shake her hand, but she brushed it aside and put her arms around his neck. For a moment he held her there, and his lips met hers in a silent farewell. It put a spell on Rainbow, and he was halfway to Vernal before Grumpy could get a word out of him.

"That girl hit you pretty hard, didn't she?" the little one questioned with unexpected softness.

"We won't go into that," Rainbow answered tightly "This fiddle-footed business we're in unfits a man for some things."

By the time they were ready to leave town, two days later, Howie was able to ride. Together they started north. In the afternoon they pulled up at Ute Crossing. The place looked as dilapidated as ever. Out in back a young Ute squaw was washing clothes.

"Yampa, where are you?" Grumpy bellowed as they stepped into the deserted barroom.

The old man came hurriedly. He was dressed in new raiment of startling pattern.

"Name it, boys!" Yampa grinned. "This round is on me!"

"Yampa, you look like a million dollars," Rainbow de-

189

clared, a twinkle in his gray eyes. "Is everything all right here?"

"Shore is, Rip! Couldn't be better! I'm makin' some improvements. Goin' to have new glass put in the winders tomorrow. New stock o' drinkables comin' too. That's for the fancy trade; I can mix it up myself for the Utes."

The two partners had a drink with him. Moran had treated him handsomely, Yampa told them.

"What about that young squaw out in back?" Grumpy demanded suspiciously.

"Why, that's the new missus," the old man cackled. "I got rid of ole Jennie. She didn't fit in with prosperity. "I give her a hunderd dollars, an' she was married off to a Ute buck inside o' three hours."

Rainbow shook his head reprovingly. "You're a shameless old man, Yampa."

"Reckon I am," was the grinning answer. "I'm smart, too."

When they were leaving, Yampa walked to the door with them and stood watching until a shoulder of the mountain hid them from view.

"There goes a couple o' high-class gents," he muttered as he turned away. "Rip and Grump are a nice pair o' boys when yuh get to know 'em!"

Bliss Lomax was a pseudonym for **Harry Sinclair Drago**, born in 1888 in Toledo, Ohio. Drago quit Toledo University to become a reporter for the Toledo *Bee*. He later turned to writing fiction with *Suzanna: A Romance Of Early California*, published by Macauley in 1922. In 1927 he was in Hollywood, writing screenplays for Tom Mix and Buck Jones. In 1932 he went East, settling in White Plains, New York, where he concentrated on writing Western fiction for the magazine market, above all for Street & Smith's *Western Story Magazine*, to which he had contributed fiction as early as 1922. Many of his novels, written under the pseudonyms Bliss Lomax and Will Ermine, were serialised prior to book publication in magazines. Some of the best of these were also made into films. The Bliss Lomax titles *Colt Comrades* (Doubleday, Doran, 1939) and *The Leather Burners* (Doubleday, Doran, 1940) were filmed as superior entries in the Hopalong Cassidy series with William Boyd, *Colt Comrades* (United Artists, 1943) and *Leather Burners* (United Artists, 1943). At his best Drago wrote Western stories that are tightly plotted with engaging characters, and often it is suspense that comprises their pulse and dramatic pacing.